FIGHTING ROUGH

A POST-APOCALYPTIC EMP SURVIVAL
THRILLER - THE EMP BOOK 5

RYAN WESTFIELD

Copyright © 2018 by Ryan Westfield

All rights reserved.

No part of this book may be reproduced in any form or by any electronic or mechanical means, including information storage and retrieval systems, without written permission from the author, except for the use of brief quotations in a book review.

Any resemblance to real persons living or dead is purely coincidental. All characters and events are products of the author's imagination.

Stock image for cover provided by Neo Stock.

1

MAX

James had been hunting for mushrooms on his own yesterday. He'd become the resident mushroom expert.

The rest of them, Max included, had been back at camp when James had come sprinting back, urgency on his face. He'd been so out of breath that he'd been unable to speak at first.

They'd all seen on his face that something was wrong. Very wrong.

"There's someone here," he'd finally said. "Someone from the compound. Less than a mile away."

"The compound?" Max had said. "Are you sure?"

James had nodded vigorously.

"How do you know?"

"I recognized him. He was in the dining hall with us when we were there."

"How can you be sure, though?" said Jake.

"He's got a good memory for faces," said Sadie.

"I would have just shot him," said James. "But if there

was someone else, I would have just drawn attention to us."

"You did the right thing."

It had been a blow to everyone. For the last week, they'd enjoyed an unusual sense of calm at their makeshift camp set up near Jake and Rose's parked van. No one else knew they were there. They wanted to keep it that way.

It had been close to sundown, and they'd decided it'd be best to set out to investigate the following day. They'd doubled the watch, put out the fire, and suffered through the cold night.

No one had slept much, and when the morning had come, they were all tired and weak from lack of sleep.

"Thanks," said Max, accepting the mug of coffee that Rose handed him.

He held the hot mug and took a sip of the strong, bitter coffee. It filled him with some much-needed warmth.

It was unusually cold. Winter had come early, and the air temperature was below freezing. Their water had frozen overnight.

"Looks like it might snow," said John, looking up to the grey clouds that stretched across the entire sky.

"Let's hope not," said Max. "We don't need any more problems. Although..."

"What is it?"

"If there's someone snooping around our area, snowfall could be a huge help."

"You're talking about the tracks?"

"Yeah, we'll be able to see easily enough if someone's been here."

John nodded thoughtfully as he chewed his venison.

Venison was practically their only food, aside from the mushrooms James hunted.

Their group was bigger than it had been. John and Cynthia, and Jake and Rose had joined their group less than a week ago. They'd all pooled their food together. But there really hadn't been much. John had explained how they'd had to ditch most of their food when on the run from the militia scouts.

There'd been some food at the pot farmers tent. They'd had a stockpile of canned foods, along with long-lasting foods like rice and beans. But they'd all agreed that the best thing to do was save the shelf-stable items until they really needed it. If at some point in the future they couldn't get venison, they'd be glad they'd saved the food. For now, the deer were plentiful. They'd shot two over the last week.

Max finished his portion of venison, drained the last of his coffee, and nodded to Mandy. "Come on," he said. "Let's get moving."

"Almost ready," said Mandy, not even glancing up. She was checking her rifle.

They finally had ammunition for their rifles. Not a lot. But some. The pot farmers had been fairly well armed. They'd even had ammunition for guns they didn't have with them.

"You sure you don't want me to come?" said John.

Max shook his head. "Better to have you here."

John nodded.

"Ready," said Mandy, shouldering her rifle.

She and Max set off, heading north, into the woods. They walked in silence for the first ten minutes.

The air seemed to be getting colder. Max had on his

jacket, but it was far from being a winter jacket. At least they were moving. That was the best way to stay warm.

When the cold was really bad was at night. Especially without the fire. They had some sleeping bags and blankets. But not enough.

The group's gear was really a hodgepodge. Bits and pieces. Nothing was complete. The things John and Cynthia had brought had been scavenged from various other peoples' gear, and then they'd had to abandon half of it.

The things taken from the pot farmers had been useful, but obviously the pot farmers hadn't been preparing for an event like this. They were just expecting to be out in the woods for a month or so, with regular trips into town, judging from what they'd had with them.

Jake and Rose were a whole different situation altogether. They'd had some invaluable things, like the radio. Not to mention a working van. And some treats, like plenty of coffee. But they had no guns, no knives. Nothing but basic camping gear.

A larger group had plenty of advantages. And a lot more problems.

More mouths to feed, more people to worry about.

Max walked along, lost in his own thoughts, his eyes scanning the cold forest.

Finally, Mandy spoke.

"Aren't you happy to see your brother again?"

"Of course," said Max. "Why?"

Frankly, the question puzzled him.

"You haven't seemed happy since he got here. And you hardly talk to him. He clearly wants to talk to you."

Max shrugged. "We're trying to survive," he said.

"There's no time for happiness. We're either alive or we're not."

"But you know what I mean. He's your brother. I hardly hear you two talking. Was that how your family was or something?"

"I'm not going to get into my whole family history," said Max. "It's not important. Not now. Keep your eyes open for anything unusual."

"Nothing so far," said Mandy. "I just don't get the thing between you and John."

Max sighed. "Fine," he said. "You really want my thoughts on it?"

Mandy nodded. "It's like prying nails sometimes with you. Go ahead. Please."

"We weren't that close," said Max. "I'm happy he's alive, obviously. He's very different now than he was. The EMP changed him. Probably for the better. I think he can be a big help to us."

"Real deep," muttered Mandy.

Max shrugged and looked to the sky. A single snowflake fell onto his nose.

"Snow," said Max. "I guess John was right."

"I hate the snow," muttered Mandy. "Makes me thinks of having to shovel out my car. And dealing with traffic."

"Well, that's not going to be a problem. Although the roads could get bad without anybody plowing. Depends how much it snows."

"Hopefully it doesn't come to having to deal with that. I'm liking having a camp, a home base. Rather than being on the move."

"Me too," said Max. "But it doesn't really matter what we like."

"Yeah," said Mandy, finishing his thought for him. "It's

about what keeps us alive. You've told us all countless times."

Over the next hour, they traveled in a large arc around the campsite. There were no signs of anyone. The snow continued to fall. It was picking up, and showed no signs of slowing down. Soon, there was a light covering of snow on the ground.

"We're making tracks," said Max, pointing down to their footprints.

"I don't know if that's good or bad."

"Could be both."

"We never talked about what we're going to do if we find someone out here," said Mandy. "Are we just going to shoot them dead? After all, we can't let the compound know we're here. I'm not hesitating this time. I'm not going to let that stuff get to me again. My trigger finger's ready. No hesitation."

She was talking rapidly, as if she was trying to convince herself more than she was trying to convince Max.

"Don't go trigger happy. We need information," said Max. "As they say, dead men can't talk."

"Information? You mean if they know we're here or not."

"Exactly."

They were both covered with a light dusting of snow that slowly grew as they walked.

"The forest seems so peaceful with the snow," remarked Mandy.

"It's not going to take much to change that..."

Suddenly, Mandy put her hand up.

Max fell silent.

Mandy stopped in her tracks, slightly ahead of Max.

She was peering off to the east. Max didn't see anything, so he put his binoculars to his eyes and adjusted them as he scanned the snow-covered trees.

"I saw movement," whispered Mandy.

"I'm not seeing anything," said Max.

He put the binoculars down. Mandy had her rifle's scope to her eye.

"I'm not either now," said Mandy. "Maybe it was just an animal."

"There are plenty of places to hide," said Max. "If there's someone out there, they had every chance to see us if you saw them."

"What do we do?"

"We wait."

"You think there's someone out there, just staying still, behind a tree or something?"

"Exactly."

"What if it was just an animal?"

"We can't take the risk. I'll use the binoculars. Don't use your scope for now. Keep your eyes over there, but I need you looking around too. There's a chance they snuck off and will come at us from another side."

The minutes passed, and there was no more movement. The snow continued to fall, and the temperature was dropping further.

Max checked his watch, and hoped that those back at camp were keeping a good watch.

2

JOSH

The snow was falling heavily now, and Josh shivered in the cold. He had on a large white parka, as well as a heavy Russian-style hat, and good, heavy boots. He was even wearing a merino wool sweater. It should have been enough to keep him warm. But he hadn't eaten enough. His metabolism had slowed down, and his body wasn't generating much heat.

They'd seen him. There were two of them. A man and a woman. Both were armed. He hadn't gotten a look at their faces. Was it Max? Someone else?

Josh had his back flat against the tree trunk. The trunk was cold, and seemed to sap more heat from his body.

Surely they had at least one rifle trained on his position.

If he moved away from the tree, he'd be shot.

Josh clutched his own rifle, holding it tightly with his stiff hands. One piece of important gear he was missing were gloves thin enough that he could operate a gun.

Josh tried to keep his mind on the task at hand. But

there was nothing to do. The only way to stay alive was not to move. And not to make any noise.

His mind started to wander as he remembered the events that had led up to him being out there, alone in the snowy woods, possibly about to die.

Josh was one of the few at the compound who hadn't had an interest in disaster preparedness before the EMP. But his best friend had always been talking about it, and, at the time, Josh had been unemployed. He'd joined mostly because he'd needed something to do with his time. He'd never seriously thought that an event like the EMP would happen.

Now Dan was dead. Along with Kara. And a handful of others. And that didn't even include the ones Max and his gang had killed.

The atmosphere in the compound had changed drastically. And rapidly. They'd been a fairly amiable group of guys at first.

Now, there was a thread of viciousness that ran through them all. They wanted revenge. They wanted someone to pay for their dead. They'd all lost friends, people they'd lived with and worked with.

The founding members of the compound had, with the exception of Josh, generally believed that they were planning the rest of their lives. Before the EMP, the compound had been a sort of fantasy that they fully expected to actually play out. But it had been more of a fantasy. It had been escapism in its best form. It'd been a way to get through the dull day jobs, and the monotony and drudgery of office life, of dead end jobs with low pay. They'd known they were different, that they were prepared.

That spirit had lived on past the EMP. Sure, the reality

had been different than a lot of them had imagined. It'd been harsher, for one thing. The comforts of civilized life were no longer an option, no longer just a drive away. There was no going back.

But now, the dream had been shattered. The attack by Max's group, along with Kara's death, had splintered the dream into mere fragments. Sure, Kara herself had been changing the overall attitude. But Max had changed everything.

They'd all been willing to defend themselves, to use violence if necessary. But it had been thought of and talked about as a last resort.

Now, they were bloodthirsty.

When the scout from some militia had showed up, he'd been accepted with open arms. If he'd arrived a couple weeks ago, he would have been met with nothing but skepticism.

Instead, they all seemed eager to join forces with a militia, a group that ruled with force and violence and nothing else. It was the opposite of the principles of shared worked on which the compound had been founded.

Josh, and Josh alone, had remained skeptical. He'd stood in the shadows, in the corners, listening and not talking much.

To Josh, the militia obviously didn't have the compound's best interest at heart. They wanted to use them for their own ends.

And what did the militia want?

They wanted more power. They wanted new allies. As well as to expand into new territories.

The chaos and violence of anarchy was bad enough.

Was a vicious military-ruled government really any better? Josh didn't think so.

The militia was looking for certain pieces of technology. Things that still worked. Things that could be used in their conquests.

They wanted more radios, for one thing.

Josh had been there when the compound members had been showing Devon, the militia scout, their own radio. He'd been impressed that it still worked, and had wanted a demonstration.

That's when they'd overheard the discussion between the two brothers, Max and John. It'd been one week ago to the day. Max had foolishly given away his position, so that his brother could come join him.

That had been everything they'd needed to know. Almost.

Max hadn't given his exact position. More like a set of directions on how to find him. He'd been somewhat vague, perhaps knowing that it was possible others were listening.

If so, then he'd been clever. He'd given his brother a meeting place that wasn't exactly the location of their camp.

The compound almost knew where Max was, and that he had one radio. And that his brother was coming with yet another.

It was too good of an opportunity to pass up.

Josh hadn't wanted to go. He'd stayed in the corner, not speaking, hoping they'd forget about him.

But Johnson had volunteered himself, and then Josh along with them. They were to act as the scouting party.

The mission? Find Max's exact location, leave unnoticed, and report back. In the meantime, the compound had other matters to attend to.

Josh looked up.

Johnson was walking towards him in his big white parka and his snowcap. Apparently he was unaware that there were two others here. He hadn't seen them yet.

Josh waved his hand furiously at Johnson.

Johnson paused, looking confused.

He wasn't known for being the brightest. He wore a confused expression on his face as he looked at Josh's waving hand.

The crack of a rifle sounded through the frigid air.

Johnson let out a scream, falling to the ground.

Josh couldn't tell if Johnson was dead or not. But he knew he couldn't do anything for him. If he ran out there, he'd be shot, too.

Another crack.

Johnson was returning fire. He wasn't dead. Not yet. He'd crawled on his belly behind a fallen tree trunk.

Johnson was firing at irregular intervals. For now, it seemed like the enemies weren't returning fire.

This was Josh's chance.

He didn't want to die.

Not like this. Not here.

If he stayed to fight, it meant relying on his own abilities. And Johnson's. And frankly, he didn't put much trust in either.

No, he wouldn't fight. He'd do the cowardly thing. The smart thing.

He'd save his own life.

Holding his rifle in one hand, Josh dashed out from behind the tree, running away from Johnson and the enemies. His legs were so cold, he worried he wouldn't be able to actually run very fast. But he warmed up as he ran.

With each breath he took, and each step, he expected to feel the bullet that would kill him.

But nothing happened. No bullet found him.

He ran and he ran, until he couldn't run anymore.

He ran until he couldn't hear the gunshots.

He'd left it all behind.

He didn't know if Johnson had survived. Probably not, though. He was kind of a moron, always making mistakes with simple chores back at the compound. They were only friends out of desperation and nothing more. Lack of better company, to put it nicely.

The snow was falling fast and heavy. His boots made tracks in the snow.

What should he do now?

Exhausted, he sat down in the snow, not caring if he got snow on the seat of his pants.

Should he return to the compound?

Probably.

Probably Johnson was dead, and wouldn't be able to tell anyone that Josh had fled, rather than fought.

But Josh still hadn't found Max's camp. He couldn't return to the compound empty-handed, without any information.

Though the thought of trudging on, and probably getting killed for it, didn't seem appealing in any sense.

He didn't want to get shot just to find out where Max's camp was. What was the point of it all? Josh didn't see any personal benefit to it. It just seemed like they'd be helping the militia and Josh would get nothing in return. He'd still be eating the same food day in and day out, not to mention freezing his ass off every night and day.

What if he just made up the information? Told them a spot on the map that seemed likely. That would work until they sent the attack party out. Then again, maybe they'd just think Max and his group had moved on, rather than blaming Josh for lying. But, no, that wouldn't work because there wouldn't be any signs of a campground. When the attack party eventually came back to the compound, disappointed, they'd know who to blame.

And they'd probably kill him.

There wasn't any good way out.

But at least he wasn't going to die right then and there, like Johnson probably had, riddled with bullets.

The woods were large, and he felt safe there in the snow.

He gazed out at the calm, peaceful woods. Before the EMP, this would have been an idyllic scene worthy of vacation photos and internet posts. But now...

Well, it still seemed peaceful. The snow had a way of making everything seem quieter. There wasn't a single animal sound.

Josh's gaze moved steadily around his surroundings. He was trying to enjoy it, trying to find some brief period of calm before he had to figure how what his next move was.

And that was when he noticed the footprints.

His footprints. They were as clear as day in the snow. His eyes followed the trail, which led back to the scene of the shootout.

Shit.

They'd find him.

If they wanted him, all they had to do was follow the trail. And it would lead them straight back to Josh.

He could keep running, maybe try to conceal his footprints somehow. But it seemed like it'd be a losing battle. By the time he got a pine branch and started brushing, they'd already be there. If they were after him, that is. And they certainly would be.

If it had been Max, he had every reason to try to protect the secrecy of his location. Maybe he realized he'd made a blunder on the radio. Or maybe he didn't. Either way, he must have known that he was less likely to attract trouble if no one knew he was there.

It was a tough choice to make. Especially for a coward.

Josh had no problems admitting he was a coward. Not to himself, at least.

But that self-admission did make it hard to decide to stay and fight. Something about it seemed contradictory.

Josh found a place where he thought he might remain somewhat concealed. His white parka definitely was an advantage. The compound had the advantage of owning some specialty gear. That was what planning did for you. Not many other groups or individuals would have had such foresight.

Josh positioned his rifle so he'd have a clear shot, straight down the path of his footprints.

Then he waited, shivering in the cold, his finger on the trigger, and snow falling around him.

3

JAMES

"You get enough to eat, Mom?" said James.

"Thanks, James, I'm fine," said Georgia.

She was looking a lot better. Some color had returned to her face, and she'd started walking around the camp. It might still be a while, though, before she was out hunting again. And she was itching to do it. But the walks had quelled some of her frustration.

"You warm enough?"

"I'm fine, James. Don't worry about me."

"You sure?"

"Of course. Now go do something useful with yourself."

Georgia continued walking, unaided, along her small path that circled the camp. Neither the snow or the freezing temperatures were going to deter her.

James looked out at the snow-covered trees and wondered about Max and Mandy.

But, as Max would have said, there was no point in worrying about something he couldn't change. The thing to do was keep going. And the meaning of that was always situationally-dependent.

In this moment, it meant defending and readying the camp.

John and Sadie were on watch. They were positioned at opposite ends of the camp, waiting and watching in the cold.

James had the brotherly instinct to go check on Sadie, but at the last moment, he thought better of it. After all, he knew she'd be fine. She was bundled up plenty, and more likely she'd just talk his ear off complaining about being bored and about being cold.

Most of the work that the camp needed had already been done over the last week. Together, they'd taken the tent from the pot farmers and brought it over to Jake and Rose's van. With one person always on watch, the van and the tent together provided enough sleeping space for everyone. Not that either structure did much against the cold.

James had argued that they should just move the van now that they had gasoline. But Max had pointed out that the fields of marijuana weren't something they wanted to live very close to. He'd said it be better if they could move farther away, but that it'd be too inconvenient. The fields, Max had said, could draw unwanted attention. It was, after all, a resource that some might potentially be after.

The fire was still out, so as not to draw more attention. There was enough food for now, and James knew he couldn't go hunting anyway. Not with someone potentially being out there.

It bothered James to have no immediate project. Nothing to help with.

Max's brother was inside the tent, fiddling with the

radio that he'd brought. Now they had two radios. And no one to communicate with.

"What you doing?" said James.

"Oh, just trying to figure out how we can continue to power this thing."

"The battery won't last?"

John shook his head. "Nope," he said. "In fact, the battery for the one I brought is already dead."

"What about the one from Jake and Rose?"

"They've got it rigged up to a car battery," said John. "It's got more juice. But not a lot. I'm trying to figure out how to attach it to the car. You know anything about that sort of thing?"

James shook his head. "Not really," he said.

"That's the thing with people your age," said John.

"What do you mean?"

"Before the EMP, everything was just a quick internet search away. You never had to know anything."

"Same goes for you, too," said James, feeling himself grow a little defensive. He didn't yet know John very well. And while he seemed like a good guy, he hadn't yet earned James's respect the way Max had.

John laughed. "You're right," he said. "I mean, look, I don't know how to do this either. I got so used to my smartphone, I bet I forgot most of what I ever learned. I guess we're going to have to get used to it. I don't think there's any going back."

"So you don't think the US can restart again?"

John shrugged. "I don't know. I don't think I'm as pessimistic as Max is, from the sound of it. But I'm getting there, I guess. What about you?"

"I don't know," said James. "From what I've seen... the

way people are acting... it'd take something pretty... I don't know... crazy to get everything back in order."

John nodded. The conversation gradually dwindled down, as John went back to work fiddling with the bits of wiring he was hoping to use to charge the batteries for the radio.

James found himself outside again, staring at the grey sky. The snow was really coming down.

He knew he wasn't supposed to leave camp, but he hated not having something useful to do.

The firewood was all ready. For when they wanted to make a fire, that is. The guns were as clean as they could. Everything was in order.

But what about the pot farmers camp? They'd taken the tent and some other food. But James was convinced that there must still be something there that could be useful to them. After all, those men hadn't seemed like the most organized. Surely they would have been the types to leave valuables around in odd places.

James glanced to his left and then his right. For the moment, everyone was occupied.

James slipped away from camp, heading towards the old pot farm.

His shoes made prints in the snow as he walked swiftly, leaning in against the cold wind. The heavy snow soon made the camp invisible when he glanced back at it. Good, no one would notice that he was gone.

4

MAX

"I think I could have gotten him with a cleaner shot," said Mandy.

"It was a good shot," said Max. "It did the job."

"Yeah, but I think… you know, I just want to make sure I've still got it, that I can do what I need to do."

She hadn't stopped talking about killing the man since it'd happened ten minutes ago. She seemed to be trying to convince herself that she wasn't going to be weak, that she was able to kill when it was necessary.

Finally, Max had to put a stop to it.

"Listen, Mandy," he said. "I know you were dealing with some shit. But talking about it isn't going to change it. You either do what you need to do or you don't. And you did it. It was a good shot, and that's that."

Mandy fell silent.

"The snow's falling heavier now," said Max. "I don't know how long we have before the snow covers up these tracks completely. Come on, let's pick up the pace."

"But what happens when we find him?" said Mandy.

"We're trying to take this one alive," said Max. "If it's at all possible."

"And if not?"

"Same as the last one," said Max, running his thumb across his neck. "If he's from the compound, or the militia, we can't let him leave alive."

"I'm worried he's just at the end of these footprints, waiting, ready to shoot us."

"That's probably exactly what he's doing," said Max. "If he has any sense at all. I think this one is smarter than the last one. The visibility is so low now that I think we have the upper hand."

"Let's hope so," said Mandy.

The wind had picked up, and it was hard to see in front of them. The snow blew furiously, the wind changing direction sporadically.

They were walking across a field. If it hadn't been for the snow, they would have been easy targets.

They were coming up to the end of the field, where the tree line started again.

"If it was me," said Max. "I'd be waiting right up there in those trees."

"So what do we do?"

"Stop here. We're right past the range of his rifle. Here's what we'll do. You stay here. Keep your eyes on the woods. I'll go around from the side and cut him off. If he's there, I'll take him by surprise."

"And if he's not?"

"Then we've got to keep following him."

"We might freeze to death, Max. We can't follow him for hours and hours."

"We'll have to," said Max. "We can't let him leave."

"He doesn't even know where the camp is, remember?"

"As far as we know, and that doesn't mean much. I screwed up giving John a meeting place over the radio. I'm not going to let that mistake get us all killed."

"What were you going to do, though? You had to give John somewhere to meet you."

"There's no time to discuss that now. And we'll worry about tracking this guy later. My bet is that he's there in the woods, waiting for us."

"Are you sure about this, Max?"

Max shook his head. "No, but it's the best plan. For now. And remember, don't shoot him dead unless you really need to."

"Unless I really need to."

"Unless he's about to kill one of us, try to keep him alive. Remember, we need information."

"I don't think I'm that good of a shot, Max."

"It's not that hard. Remember, stay calm. You'll be more accurate."

"Easier said than done."

With a nod of his head, Max set off through the snow, leaving Mandy behind. He turned his head to see her getting behind a tree. Her rifle soon became the only thing visible, protruding out from the trunk.

A minute later, he couldn't see her at all. The falling snow was in the way.

Max's boots made huge deep prints in the snow. He cut a big half-circle of a path, taking the long way around so that he could come up from the east.

His hands were so cold they were stiff, so he slung his gun back over his shoulder, and stuck them in his pockets. He needed them warm for when he needed the rifle.

Max could see his breath in the air. He walked quickly, but not enough to make him actually feel warm. Just fast enough to keep him from freezing. He hoped Mandy would stay warm enough to fight effectively.

If it came to that, that is. Max was hoping he'd be able to sneak up on the guy from behind, avoiding any kind of firefight.

Of course, he knew very well that things were never as easy as he'd hope. Plans never went the right way. The smart thing to do was expect changes and adapt on the fly. Easier said than done.

Max had crossed the field, and he entered the heavily wooded area. The presence of the trees somewhat protected him against the falling snow. But there was still plenty of snow on the ground, on the trees, and in the air.

In another time, this would have been an idyllic scene. There was a certain type of quiet in the air that only comes from a fresh snowfall.

But Max wasn't paying attention to that aspect of his surroundings. His eyes were scanning the forest carefully, looking for any signs of the man.

Max was coming up from behind. Coming from the opposite direction the enemy would be expecting. Hopefully.

It was as much of a game of strategy and intelligence as anything else. Max had to outsmart the enemy in order to stay alive.

He walked slowly, bending his back, crouching, staying low to the ground.

He had his rifle out now. His hands and fingers were cold, but they'd work well enough.

Truthfully, he felt more comfortable with his Glock.

But it wasn't ideal for this sort of situation. Only the rifle could provide the range he'd need.

There was something up ahead, towards the line where the woods met the field. Max thought his eyes were playing tricks on him at first. Then he realized it was the man's white winter coat simply creating a strange illusion. It was the hat that made him visible. A big, incredibly warm looking hat, like the kind the Russian soldiers wore in old movies. It was black, and stuck out from the white snowy background like a sore thumb.

Max stopped where he was, not wanting to make any more noise.

He put his eye to his rifle's scope. The man was facing away from him, his own rifle pointed towards where Mandy was. He was definitely lying in wait. Max had been right to expect the man to be waiting for them rather than continue on.

Max took careful aim. The man's right shoulder was in Max's crosshairs. Hopefully, that'd be enough to immobilize him, and prevent him from using his rifle.

Max squeezed the trigger.

He'd hit him.

The man didn't scream. He let off a strange grunt-like noise of pain, muffled by the snow and trees.

As long as Mandy stayed where she was, she'd be safe. After all, there was a chance the man could still get off a shot.

Max darted behind a tree trunk and waited. The man's painful grunting continued, turning into an animal-like wail.

Max waited, then made his move. But not before getting his rifle back on his shoulder, and getting his Glock out and ready.

Max dashed towards the man, the Glock pointed directly at him.

"Don't make a move," Max shouted. He didn't need to worry about others in the area overhearing him. He had no need to be quiet anymore. Hopefully.

The man had dropped his gun on the snow. He was clutching his shoulder. It'd been a good shot. Max had hit him right when he'd been aiming.

The man's face was contorted in pain. But that didn't stop Max from recognizing him. James had been right.

He was from the compound.

Max pointed his Glock right at the man's face.

"One move and you're dead," said Max.

The man nodded his understanding.

"Any other weapons?"

The man shook his head.

"I've learned not to trust answers like that," said Max, using his free hand to pat the man down.

Sure enough, there was a handgun tucked into the man's waistband.

"They don't issue holsters at the compound?" said Max. "They've sure got you outfitted well for the snow."

The man said nothing.

"I need to know," said Max, "why you're here. Tell me the truth, and I'll let you live."

But Max was lying. He didn't know if he could let the man live. He didn't like playing this game, making a promise he couldn't keep. But that was what the circumstances dictated. If he let him live, he'd head back to the compound and tell them everything he knew. That was a given.

"Why should I trust you?" said the man, a terrified expression on his face.

"You shouldn't," said Max. "But you don't have any other choice."

Max looked up to see Mandy coming out of the falling snow, her body slowly becoming visible as she emerged from what looked like a moving white curtain.

"You got him?"

Max nodded.

"Anyone else here?"

"Not that I can tell. I need you to keep a lookout, though."

Mandy eyed the man, looking him up and down. "Your friend wasn't as smart as you. But you weren't smart enough."

"He's not my friend."

"What's your name?" said Max.

The man hesitated. But only for a moment. He glanced at Max's Glock, and seemed to decide that he'd have a better chance of living if he answered the questions.

"Josh."

"And you're from the compound, the same one we escaped from?"

"You mean the same one you attacked?"

"Attacked?"

"You killed a lot of good men."

"We didn't have a choice. You tried to kill me, and you were going to keep our women kidnapped there forever."

"That's not the way I heard it."

"Well you heard wrong," said Max. "Those are the facts. Now what are you doing here?"

"Just going for a walk."

Max moved fast, upper cutting Josh in the stomach with a solid punch. It gave him no pleasure to do it. But he needed answers. Real ones. He needed to show him he meant business.

Josh gasped for breath.

"Take your time catching your breath," said Max. "But the next words out of your mouth better be something real, something useful. My suspicions are that you're out here scouting our location, that you heard us on the radio, and want to come finish the job. But what doesn't make sense to me is the motive. Aside from pure revenge..."

The seconds ticked by, and Josh hadn't yet spoken.

"You'd better do as he says," said Mandy. "You seem to think he's a killer, but you don't know the half of it."

"And that is?" said Josh, a sarcastic twinkle in his eyes. He didn't seem to take her seriously.

"That I'm a lot worse." As she spoke the words, she pulled out her Mora knife. She leaned down swiftly, and pushed the tip of the knife against Josh's throat. Hard enough to draw a single spot of blood, but not hard enough to do any serious damage. She held the knife there. "One wrong move, one wrong word, and I'll thrust this knife so far into your throat that..." Her words trailed off, but the fire didn't leave her eyes.

Max gave her a quizzical look. She hadn't acted like this before. But he knew she'd been fighting with something inside herself. She'd hated the fact that she'd hesitated to kill when it had been necessary to save Max's life.

It seemed she'd gotten over it, though. She'd shot the other man from the compound. And now she didn't seem to hesitate to threaten real violence. And it wasn't an empty threat.

Max just hoped she didn't swing too far over to the other side. If she became a loose cannon, she'd just as much a danger to everyone if she was hesitant.

But it was Mandy he was thinking of. She was sensible and practical. It would take a lot for her to swing too far to the other side.

"Answer the question," hissed Mandy.

"OK. I'm from the compound, and..."

Mandy pressed the knife a little harder into his throat. Just hard enough for some blood to come trickling out. She didn't have the knife against his jugular, but that didn't mean it wasn't dangerous. "You already told us that," she said.

"Mandy..." said Max, his tone warning her against going too far.

"Damn, lady," said Josh. "Take that knife away from my throat and I'll tell you."

Max gave her a look.

"Fine," she muttered.

She pulled the knife back, but kept it close to Josh, ready to strike at any moment.

"I've been instructed to find your position. You were right, Max. They heard you on the radio. But they don't know the position of your camp."

"It's a lot of work just for revenge," said Max. "What's the end game?"

Josh started talking quickly, spilling the beans on the whole story. He told them about the man from the militia, the one who had chased John and Cynthia through the wood on a dirt bike. He told them how the militia wanted the radios, and how the compound was more than willing to team up with them.

"But what's in it for the compound?" said Max. "Just the promises from the militia?"

"Basically," said Josh. "But there's internal politics going on. Since Kara's death, it's been chaotic. I don't like the way things are going... they forced me to come, Max... I didn't want to do it. I'm not like the others, you've got to believe me..."

"Just tell the rest of the story," said Max. "You said Kara's dead. What's happening in her place?"

"New people are vying for power," said Josh. "There's a guy named Anton. He'll lead the raiding party if I go back with your position. Not that I'm going to do that, Max. You've got to believe me. Let me live, and I'll... Well, I'd join you if you'd let me."

"We'll worry about that later," said Max. "Just out with the information. Nothing more. OK?"

"You heard him," said Mandy, waiving the knife threateningly.

Max shook his head briefly at her, indicating for her to cut it out. That kind of behavior wasn't going to get them anywhere. The threat of the Glock was already there.

Josh glanced up at Max.

"Info," said Max. "Now."

"OK, OK. Anyway, Anton is looking to lead the raiding party. He thinks he'll be able to gain power within the compound by doing so, as well as strengthen his own personal ties with the envoy from the militia. I doubt it'll work, but that's what he's intending... Now if you'll just hear me out, I have a lot to offer you guys."

"Anything more I should know?" said Max.

"Anything more?"

"If you're hoping to join us, I'd think you'd want to give us all the information possible. Information that would help keep us alive."

"Ah, well, of course. No, that's about everything."

"OK, now I need you to be quiet," said Max. "While we figure out what to do with you."

"Don't kill me," pleaded Josh, still clutching his shoulder. "Please don't."

Tears were streaming down from his eyes, and his face contorted into a desperate wail.

Max's own face remained unchanged. He didn't take his eyes off Josh.

"Not one more word," said Max.

Max wasn't cruel, but he also didn't trust Josh. After all, he was a stranger, a man from the compound. And he had every reason to lie to save his own skin.

"So what do we do with him?" said Max.

"Kill him," said Mandy. "There's no other way. If he goes back to the compound, we're dead."

"What if he's telling the truth?"

"About what?"

"About wanting to join us. We could use someone like him."

"Someone like him? A killer from the compound? The same people who tried to kill us? Are you going soft, Max?"

"I'm trying to be rational," said Max. "That's not the same as going soft. You don't want to go too hard, either, Mandy."

"Don't listen to her, Max," said Josh, who hadn't stopped crying. "There's no reason to kill me. I could help you guys out. I could tell you everything the compound knows..."

Max wasn't being soft in considering keeping the guy alive. He was thinking about the survival of himself, Mandy, Georgia, and the others.

If he had to kill him, he would. Plenty of "innocent" people had died already. And plenty more would soon enough.

And Josh's innocence was highly suspect.

The snow hadn't let up. Instead, it was falling heavier now than ever.

And the temperature was dropping. Max felt the cold. Especially his leg. The cold seemed to aggravate his injury.

The sun was completely blotted out by the snow. Max raised his wrist to check the time, so as not to take his eyes off Josh. It was almost noon.

5

ANTON

"I don't get it," said Marshal, trudging through the snow beside Anton. "Why'd you send out those two scouts if you wanted to just roll on out yourself?"

"Easy," said Anton. "I knew those two morons would botch the whole thing. They'll work as a distraction more than anything else."

"But we still don't know where the camp is."

"It won't be hard to find. Trust me. You saw the maps."

"I did, and it's a big park."

"Hunting grounds," said Anton, correcting him. "It's not a park."

"Whatever it is, it's going to be hard to find them. Especially in this snow. I don't see why we couldn't have waited until this all blows over."

Anton chuckled. "You've got a lot to learn, Marshal. You've spent too much of your life in prison."

"Didn't have much of a choice."

"Well, watch and learn. The snow gives us cover. Decreased visibility is our friend here. We'll be able to create confusion, and cut them off when they try to flee. We'll get them, one by one. And the best thing of all? The roads are impassable, and traveling on foot far will be difficult."

"That's exactly what I'm worried about," said Marshal. "If you didn't notice, we're traveling long distances in the very same snow."

Anton made a dismissive noise. "We're outfitted perfectly for the conditions. How you liking those new boots, anyway?"

"They're fine," said Marshal, who glanced behind them.

The men from the compound walked behind them in a single file line. They all wore large parkas and heavy snow boots. And most importantly, they all carried weapons. Some had hunting rifles with scopes. But most had semi-automatic assault rifles.

Max and his pitiful little group would be no match for them.

Anton was pleased with himself. Frankly, he didn't care about the radios that they were supposedly after. What he cared about was proving himself a leader, taking control of the compound in Kara's absence. He needed to show Marshal what his group was made of, and what he himself was capable of.

Marshal may not have known much about fighting in a rural environment. But he wasn't a fool. And he'd done fine enough on the dirt bike.

Anton would have never let on, but he was terrified of Marshal. And eager to please and impress him. His bravado was merely a cover for the insecurity he felt.

Marshal had spent the last ten years of his life incarcerated. The EMP had meant a new life for him. He'd been a higher up in one of the more prominent prison gangs, and he'd used his connections to work his way up in the newly formed post-EMP militia. He'd been chosen as an envoy because of his intelligence and ability to simply "get shit done," as he put it.

Marshal was covered in prison tattoos, running in every direction across his pasty pale skin. Not that they were visible now. But Anton had seen them when they were changing into their outdoor winter gear.

"I can't see shit in this snow," said Marshal.

"Neither can the enemy," said Anton. "Our ears are our ally in a situation like this."

"Yeah, but I'd prefer seeing. You know, in prison, everything's up close and personal. You may not know what's going to happen, but at least you can see ten feet in front of you."

"Must be weird being out again, eh?" said Anton.

Marshal grunted.

"You really think we can find them in this snow? We've been on the move for what, eight hours?"

Anton glanced at his watch. "More like twelve. But we'll find them."

"How do you even know where we are?"

"I used to hunt here as a kid. That's why I know we'll find them. I don't even need to look at the maps."

"Well, let's hope nothing happens to you then, buddy, because I don't know how the hell to get out of here."

"Nothing's going to happen to me. They don't stand a chance against us."

"I hope you're right."

"I thought you'd be tougher." Anton paused, realized he might just have put his foot in his mouth.

Marshal gave him a look. It wasn't much, but it scared

Anton, making his heart start to beat faster. He was, after all, terrified of Marshal and what he was capable of.

It was funny the way it went sometimes, thought Anton. If someone had been listening to their conversation, it would have sounded like Anton was the tough one, not to mention sure of himself. But in reality, Marshal had already seen more action in his life than Anton could even dream of.

"I didn't mean it like that," said Anton. "I just meant... I thought you wouldn't be worried about their chances. You've done a lot of fighting. And before you went to prison, you were in plenty of gun fights, right?"

"That's right," said Marshal. "But if there's one thing my life has taught me, it's never underestimate your enemy."

"Words of wisdom, definitely," said Anton, glancing back at his men, who were following dutifully behind them.

"Can I ask you something?" said Marshal.

"Sure."

"Where are you from, anyway?"

"I'm from around here. What do you mean?"

"Your accent. You sound kind of foreign or something."

"Oh," said Anton. "I came here with my parents when I was ten. I grew up here, though."

"Where are you parents from?"

"Germany. They were doctors."

Anton was surprised at the question, but he shouldn't have been. After all, for one reason or another, he had never lost his German accent. It was still just as strong as his father's.

"You ever get to visit Germany? I hear it's beautiful.

One of my cellies was from there. He said there's nothing like it. Rolling green hills and all that."

"Uh, once or twice. When my grandparents died. Why are we talking about this anyway?"

It seemed strange to Anton that Marshal would be interested in his accent or his history. After all, none of that mattered now. For all Anton knew, there were no more nations. Germany could have easily gone the way the US had, crumbling into anarchy.

What he was concerned about was taking a piece of the chaos and molding it with his own sheer force of will. He wanted to exert his power over others. He wanted to bring back some law and order, no matter what the cost.

In Anton's mind, that was how the great nations had been created in the first place. Violence and power had been necessary. Required, even. Those times had fallen to the wayside, and a new era had taken over. But now the time for violence was back. This was the time for strong men, for men who weren't afraid to do what needed to be done. Order needed to be restored.

But if Anton was being honest with himself, he would have admitted that it was more than just order he wanted. He was more concerned with making his own mark, with carving his own little place in history. By whatever means necessary, of course. But wasn't that how the great nations had been founded in the first place? There'd been men who'd been willing to do whatever it took. And more often than not they'd had their own personal interests in mind rather than the interests of the greater good.

"Hey, Anton!"

Someone behind him was tapping him on the shoulder. It broke him out of his little philosophical daydream.

It was Nick, and he was pointing over to the right.

"What is it?"

"Check it out. Looks like something man made. Thought you should know."

"Let's take a look."

It was hard to tell what it was with all the snow. But it was something, a vague white blur off in the distance, barely visible through the snowfall.

"Marshal, come on."

Marshal nodded.

"OK, Nick, you come with me and Marshal. The rest of you, post up around the area. Groups of two. And don't get too far you can't see each other. I want the area covered, but I don't want any of you getting lost in the blizzard."

The three of them moved on out towards the objects. Anton lead the way. He didn't want to be like other leaders who stayed behind and let their troops do the dirty work. No, he wanted to be out there, exposing himself to danger. He wanted to get his hands dirty, to fire the first shots. His goal, after all, was to gain respect.

And the only way to do that?

Be more vicious and ruthless than anyone else.

As soon as he got his hands on Max, he'd tear into him with his own hands if he had too.

"What the hell is that?" said Marshal, from behind him.

Now that they were getting closer, the object was coming into view better. It wasn't actually an object.

"Looks like a field of some sort," said Anton. "You think that's corn someone's growing?"

"Dunno, but I'm going to find out," said Marshal, who picked up his pace, passing Anton.

Anton huffed with annoyance. After all, he wanted to be the first there. That was how it was supposed to work.

He was the leader, not Marshal. Marshal was just along for the ride, a member of a different organization altogether.

Anton's legs were aching from the hours of walking. But they were warm, and he pushed his muscles, picking up the pace. His heavy boots slogged through the snow as he struggled to keep up with Marshal, who was already more than ten feet ahead of him, rapidly approaching the snow-covered crop field.

6

JAMES

James moved slowly through the pot farmers campsite. There wasn't really much there. They'd already taken almost everything back to their own camp.

But James was convinced there had to be something of value there. Some forgotten tool. Or maybe another gun.

A box of spare ammunition would be great. It wasn't like they had an endless supply. And James was already worried about the bullets lasting through the winter. In a post-EMP world, there was no mass manufacturing. No more bullets were being produced. And the ones that were left, well, they were being used up. Probably at a rapid rate.

Bullets were commodities now. But it wasn't like they could go easy on their supply. If a threat presented itself, a bullet was usually the answer. The option to not shoot, not "waste" a bullet, simply didn't exist.

Not in the world they lived in now.

James wasn't the only one worried. Max and Georgia had had a serious discussion about setting up traps for deer. If they could spare the bullets used for hunting, it would get them a lot farther. The problem was that getting a deer snare to actually work was a lot harder than it sounded.

James suddenly realized that he should have gone to check the deer snares he and Max had set up yesterday.

For some reason, it hadn't been on his mind.

Maybe he'd just been too intent to sneak off on his own. And to make some unique discovery that would impress the others.

After all, how cool would it have been if he'd found something at the camp they'd overlooked? Something incredibly useful.

But he felt stupid now. He felt like he'd been thinking of just himself, and not of the others.

After all, getting a deer snare to work would be of greater use to them all. Killing a deer without a bullet? That was just what they needed.

Feeling foolish, James decided then and there to turn back.

He was on the other side of the snow-covered pot field, and decided to go around the camp, rather than heading back through it.

Visibility was low. The snow was getting high. James didn't have boots, just the high-top sneakers he'd worn to school. Snow was getting into them now, and his feet were freezing.

Max had lectured them on the dangers of frostbite. James could almost hear Max's voice now, telling him that he'd already made one mistake today. The important thing, Max would have said, is not to make another.

James decided to head straight back to camp, rather than going out to check on the snare.

James could hardly see anything. He hoped he was heading in the right direction. He knew it'd be easy to get turned around in this snow. He wondered briefly whether this would count as a blizzard or not.

As far as James was concerned, it was a blizzard. And what was a "blizzard," after all, but a technical classification that the television weather people slapped onto a storm.

A snowstorm was a snowstorm. It was either mild, bad, or severe. What you called it didn't really matter.

Up ahead, in the wall of white snow, something suddenly appeared.

James stopped dead in his tracks.

It was a person. Standing there in the snow.

James could just see the person's outline. And the outline of some type of rifle.

Was it a friend or enemy?

James didn't have a rifle with him, and he suddenly felt naked without one. But he had the handgun that had originally come from the gate guards at the compound. It had a full magazine in it. Eight cartridges. But he didn't have a spare mag with him.

James cursed himself again.

Should he wave? Shout something? Or simply retreat?

He couldn't simply open fire. After all, it could have been Max or Mandy.

If he got closer, he'd be just as visible to the unknown person as they were to him.

Suddenly, the figure saw him. It turned towards James and shouted something. James couldn't make out the words over the wind. But he heard the voice. And it wasn't a voice he recognized. The sound was completely foreign, completely different.

He was sure that it wasn't one of his friends or family. Positive.

James acted without thinking.

He already had his handgun out and ready.

The man kept shouting. He lowered his gun, pointing it towards James.

Another figure suddenly appeared.

The shouting, the new person—it was all chaotic. It was all happening so fast.

It would have been easy to freak out. To lose his cool. His brain was running fast and wildly.

But James didn't let it get to him. He resistant the urge to lose control. Nothing would interfere with his aim more than letting it all get to him.

He took careful aim with his handgun.

He squeezed the trigger twice.

The first man fell.

The second aimed his gun.

More shouting. James didn't hear the words. It was just noise.

James's ears were ringing from the gunshots. Everything was even more muffled than before.

The wind was stronger. A powerful gust hit James in the back, almost knocking him over.

James didn't think. He just acted.

He dashed off, sprinting away from the men.

James heard the gunshots behind him. But he didn't stop. He didn't pause.

He ran as fast as he could. The wind was behind him now, seeming to urge him on, faster and faster.

For all James knew, there were more than just two men. If he didn't get away from them, he was as good as dead. He was outgunned and he knew it. He'd gotten a better look at the rifle. It wasn't a mere hunting rifle. No, it was something semi-automatic for sure.

James clutched the handgun tightly as he ran. If he let it fall, it'd be lost forever in the high snow.

It was hard running. His footing never felt stable. Any moment he might make a misstep, since he couldn't see the ground.

It happened. His sneaker hit something hard. Maybe a root. He didn't know. It didn't matter.

James fell hard, falling forward. His face hit the snow, which cushioned his fall.

There was shouting behind him. That meant there was more than one man. Probably. It sounded like someone was shouting orders, by the tone of the voice.

James couldn't lie there. Or he'd be dead.

He found the ground beneath the snow, and pushed against it. Hard, so as to turn himself over.

James was on his back. There wasn't time to get up. Not yet.

Rapidly, he brushed his hand across his face, getting the snow off his eyes.

The first thing he saw was two figures approaching.

A gust of wind blew in, sending a torrent of icy snow into the air, briefly obscuring the figures.

7

JOHN

"You don't think they've been gone a long time?" said John.

"Quit worrying already," said Cynthia. "We're new here. We don't know how things operated."

"We've been here a week already," said John. "And don't tell me I don't know my own brother."

"You said yourself you barely spoke to him in the last ten years. Or was it didn't speak at all? I don't remember."

"You've really got a way with words," said John.

"Sorry," said Cynthia. "I just get a little sarcastic when I get stressed."

"Oh yeah?" said John. "I hadn't noticed."

"Very funny," said Cynthia. "But it has been a long time. What do you think we should do?"

John shrugged his shoulders.

John and Cynthia were standing at the edge of the camp, looking out into the blizzard.

"This is a blizzard, right?"

"I guess so," said John. "Sure looks like one."

"I'm freezing," said Cynthia. "I'm going back in the tent."

"It's not much warmer in there."

"Whatever. It's better than this."

John watched Cynthia's back as she disappeared into the white mist of snow. You couldn't even see from one end of the camp to the other.

What was surprising to John wasn't just the snow, but how fast it had come on. Just this morning, when Max and Mandy had left camp, there had only been the clouds. Not a single snowflake had yet landed.

John shivered in the cold. Max and Mandy, out there somewhere, must have really been freezing. He hoped they were OK. He didn't like the idea of finally finding his brother and then losing him again. Maybe he was just worrying too much. Maybe the circumstances were making him worry.

John decided to go check in with Georgia. Despite her injury, she seemed like the most capable of everyone there. She seemed to have a good head on her shoulders. It was lucky Max had found her, from the sound of the stories he'd heard.

It had taken John a few days to get everyone's names right. For so long, it had mostly just been himself and Cynthia. Now there were all these new faces. Until a few days ago, John hadn't realized that Jake and Rose were actually just as new to the group as he and Cynthia were.

Unfortunately, Jake and Rose actually didn't seem like they'd be much help in any situation at all. They seemed to have been added to the group by default. Almost by accident. It didn't mean they were bad people. In fact, they were almost overwhelmingly friendly and open, considering the circumstances.

But they weren't who John would turn to now.

Georgia was in the tent, resting in the corner. Her eyes were half-closed, and she seemed somewhere between sleep and wakefulness.

She nodded at John as he entered.

"Close the flap," said Cynthia, glaring at the snow that blew inside, along with a gust of frigid air. "You're letting all the heat out."

"There's no heat in here," said John. He looked at Georgia. "Georgia," he said. "I wanted to talk to you for a minute."

"She's resting," said Cynthia. "She's tired. She got shot in the back, you know."

"It's fine, Cynthia," said Georgia, struggling to sit up. "I'm a hell of a lot better than I was. What's on your mind, John?"

John squatted down near Georgia. Cynthia came over from the other side too. She glanced at John, shooting him a warning look that seemed to say, "don't bother her too much. She's recuperating."

"The storm's getting really bad," said John. "I know Max and Mandy weren't expecting this when they left."

"You're worried about them?"

John nodded.

"If there's one thing I've learned since knowing Max," said Georgia. "It's that he can take care of himself."

"But something's not right," said John. "I mean, they set out hours ago. I know I sound like I'm just overly worried about my brother. And yeah, that's part of it. But I'm worried about us here at the camp too. What if something happened to Max and Mandy? What if that man James spotted is out there?"

"You're worried about an attack on the camp?"

"Something like that. I can't shake the idea that the guy who followed us on that dirt bike... well, that he might have tracked us here."

The flap to the tent opened, and another burst of cold air entered, along with plenty of snow.

It was Sadie, bundled up in a huge blanket that was wrapped tightly around her.

She looked around the tent.

"James isn't here?"

"James? I thought he was with you," said Georgia.

"No," said Sadie. "I thought he was in here."

Everyone looked at each other.

"You haven't seen him?" said Georgia.

"I'll go look outside," said John, getting up immediately.

He had his hand on his handgun as he went through the tent flap. The snow was blowing harder than ever.

John went from one end of the camp to the other. He stuck his head into the van where Jake and Rose were cuddled up together. But there was no sign of James anywhere.

John started peering at the snow, trying to make sense of the footprints, but the wind was so strong now that the only prints he could really make out were his own. And maybe some from Sadie who'd just been out there mere minutes ago.

John was about to enter the tent again when the flap opened and Georgia came hobbling out.

She had to really brace herself against the wind.

"No sign of him?" she said.

"No," said John. "I'm sorry."

John didn't know Georgia very well. He tried to read her face, to see how she would react to the news of her missing son. But he couldn't make much out. Her expression was intense, but unreadable beyond that.

"I'll get my stuff together," said John. "Cynthia and I can set out to look for him."

"No," said Georgia, shaking her head to John's surprise.

"You don't want us to go look for your son?"

"There's no way to see," said Georgia. "What good will it do?"

"That's crazy," said Cynthia. "We'll bring a compass."

"Yeah," said John. "It won't be easy. But we've got to try."

"James can take care of himself," said Georgia. "I just hope he hasn't done something stupid, like trying to find Max and Mandy himself."

John could see it in her eyes now. She was worried about her son, despite what she said. And it was killing her that she couldn't go looking for him on her own. As John understood it, she'd taken a very serious hit to the back. She was much better than she'd been, but certainly in no condition to go trudging through a blizzard's snow.

"I'm going," said John. "No discussion. I won't go far. Not far enough to get lost myself, at least. But if James is anywhere nearby, I'll find him. If he's in trouble, I'll help."

"You're not going by yourself," said Cynthia. "What's all this 'I' about? I thought it was 'we'?"

"It's a big risk," said John. "I'll go myself."

"Since when have I not done everything with you?"

"If you're insisting," said Georgia. "Then you're taking more than those handguns."

"The hunting rifles?"

Georgia shook her head. "Won't do much good in this snow. Visibility's so bad as it is."

"Then the handguns will be better, right?"

"There's a shotgun from the pot farmers you can take."

"Good," said John. "And that's where we'll start then. Maybe James went to check out the other camp."

"Everyone here's going on watch duty," said Georgia. "We'll be ready if anything happens here. I'll go get you the shotgun."

John marveled at Georgia's ability to keep it together, considering that her son was missing.

"She's a tough cookie, eh?" said Cynthia, as they watched Georgia disappear. It didn't take long since the visibility had gotten even worse.

"You sure you're coming?" said John.

"If you're going, I'm going," said Cynthia. "You think his disappearance has anything to do with your brother?"

"I doubt it. That doesn't make sense."

"But something's going on."

"Max probably just decided to wait out the storm. Maybe he couldn't find his way. He's probably holed up comfortably under some pine tree or something."

"If he can't find his way back, I hope we can."

"You've got the compass, right?"

Cynthia nodded.

"Then we'll be fine."

But John had his reservations. He wished Cynthia wasn't insistent on coming along. But he knew her well enough, and knew how stubborn she was. There was no point in even trying to talking her out of it.

John had to do it. He didn't know James well. But to John, he wasn't much more than a kid lost out there. And possibly in great danger.

8

MAX

"What are we going to do with him?" said Mandy.

"You can't kill me," wailed Josh. "You just can't."

"The snow's getting worse," said Max.

"What's that got to do with anything? We're talking about my life here. Apparently that doesn't mean anything to you."

"We're not saying that," said Mandy. "But you've got to understand that we're in a difficult position."

"Well I'm going to bleed to death while you two figure out whether or not to kill me. Sounds like you've already made up your decision, whether or not you want to admit it."

"You're not bleeding to death," said Max. "It's just a bullet wound in the shoulder."

"'Just'? Are you crazy? No wonder you didn't care about what you did to the compound. You're a ruthless killer, Max."

He spat towards Max's boots, which were buried in the snow.

"Maybe he's right," said Mandy. "Maybe it's serious."

Max gave her a look.

"Just take a look," said Josh. "At least look at the damn thing."

"Fine," said Mandy, starting to bend down to get a closer look.

"Mandy," said Max. "That's not a good idea."

"I'm just going to..."

But she never got to finish her thought.

Josh sprang forward. He moved faster than his position seemed to have allowed for.

He threw his body against Mandy's.

Mandy fell back. She let out a shout.

Josh's hands went right for her gun. He threw his whole body weight into it, trying to wrestle it from her hands.

Obviously Josh was thinking Max wouldn't dare shoot lest he hit Mandy in the process.

That was where he was wrong.

Max took careful aim. He ignored the chaos and the commotion. He ignored Josh's grunts and the scream that had come from Mandy.

He wasn't ignoring the possibility of hitting Mandy.

But he knew that he was capable of hitting Josh and Josh alone. He'd spent enough time at the target range to know his limits and his abilities.

Max squeezed the trigger.

The noise stopped all at once.

Both Josh and Mandy lay still.

But Max knew he hadn't hit Mandy. It wasn't possible.

"Mandy?"

"Help me get this asshole off me," came Mandy's muffled voice.

Max leaned down and grabbed the dead man's weight, pulling hard at the shoulders. He got the corpse off Mandy, shoving it off into the snow.

Mandy sat up, breathing heavily.

"You OK?"

Mandy nodded.

Max offered Mandy his hand, pulling her to her feet. She tried dusting the snow off her, but it had gotten in everywhere.

Max bent down and examined the corpse. He'd shot from the side, making sure that the bullet's trajectory would leave Mandy safe.

He took the warmest clothing off the corpse, and handed it to Mandy. There was blood on some of it.

"Here," said Max. "You'd better wear this."

Mandy hesitated before taking the heavy jacket from Max.

"You should wear it, Max. You just have that light jacket on."

"I'll be fine," said Max.

He knew Mandy tended to get cold more easily than he did.

Mandy nodded.

"Come on," said Max. "We've got to get a move on. We'll warm up as we walk."

They kept up a good pace at first, even though the snow was thick on the ground. But soon the constant slogging, having to really lift their boots, tired their legs out.

"We're going to have to slow down," said Mandy. "I can't keep this up."

Max nodded.

The wind blew fiercely and they had to shout to be heard by each other.

"Storm's only getting stronger," shouted Max.

"What's that?"

"Storm's getting stronger."

Mandy nodded vigorously.

The going only got harder. Soon they were too exhausted to talk, to raise their voices above the noise of the wind.

They had to walk close together, so as not to get lost.

Max couldn't see the sun, and his sense of direction was getting confused. He kept consulting his compass to make sure he was heading in the right direction.

Max's toes and fingers were starting to feel numb, despite the vigorous walking. They'd need to get back soon if they wanted to avoid frostbite. They didn't have the right winter gear to be out in a situation like this.

If there'd been such a thing as a weather report, this whole mess could have been avoided. But Max knew nothing of predicting the weather. His whole life he'd relied on the weather reports from the TV, radio, and computer. Obviously he couldn't rely on them anymore.

In city or suburban life, a blizzard was often met with a sense of annoyance or mild panic. And while there usually had been the occasional car crash or brief power outage, the overall result was usually that everything was fine. A day or so later, things were back to normal. The city plows would come in and make the roads passable again, and soon everyone would be back at work.

But now, after the EMP, everything was different. Who knew how long the snow would remain on the roads, let alone here on the ground. Max didn't know, but it might become harder to find food. They'd have to deal with the potential of plummeting temperatures, and all the physical maladies that came with that. They weren't going to be sitting out the blizzard in the relative comfort of their centrally-heated homes. No, they'd be totally immersed in it. The tent and the van provided minimal protection.

Max checked his watch. It felt like hours had passed. But it'd only been twenty minutes since he'd last checked his watch.

The hands of his analog watch gave a comforting glow in the dim light of the blizzard. It was a tough mechanical watch, Russian made, originally designed for the Russian military.

Before the age of the quartz watch, the Rolex Submariner had reigned supreme for divers. It was the only watch tough enough to hack the great depths and constant abuse of the navy divers. But the Rolex manufacturing required extremely tight tolerances that the Russians couldn't replicate in their own factories. So in typical Russian fashion, the engineers had come up with a way to achieve the same depth ratings and overall toughness of the Submariner, but for a fraction of the cost.

A wider seal, along with a domed acrylic "crystal," not to mention a robust gearing system, gave the Vostok Amphibia what it needed to compete with any other tough dive watch on the planet.

Max had always favored the watch over other, less robust modern pieces. Sure, it wasn't stylish, but it did the job. And it wasn't expensive. Max liked that about the watch.

The watch was entirely non-electronic. But Max didn't know if the standard quartz movement watches, powered by batteries, had lasted through the EMP or not. Watches weren't as popular as they had been, and no one else in his party wore one.

"You OK, Max?" said Mandy, giving his arm a tap with her fist.

"Huh?" said Max.

"You've got a glazed look on your face. I was worried I was losing you. You still with me?"

"Uh, yeah," said Max. "Just thinking about watches."

"The cold is getting to you," said Mandy. "This isn't the time for daydreaming. We've got to keep with it."

"You're right," said Max, trying to snap himself out of the little reverie he'd gotten lost in.

"Check the compass," said Mandy, pointedly.

"Right," said Max, using his numb fingers to get the compass out of his pocket again.

He didn't feel quite right, but he couldn't put his finger on what it was.

"I think the cold's affecting my brain," said Max.

"Me too," said Mandy. "And I can't feel my fingers. I hope we'll be back soon enough."

Max looked at his watch. Two hours had somehow passed. Was he losing track of time?

Max looked out into the swirling snow. He looked down at his boots, which were sunk down into the snow that reached well above the top laces. He could feel it around his socks, which were soaking wet.

"Are we headed in the right direction?"

Max checked the compass again. He felt like he was doing everything over and over. He felt like his memory was going somewhat.

He reminded himself it was just his mind playing tricks on him.

"I think we're lost, Max," said Mandy.

"No," said Max. "We can't be lost. We've been heading the right direction."

"We must have gone right past the camp," said Mandy. "We can't see anything."

A particularly strong gust of wind came, and snow blew in around them. Max braced himself against the wind, his boots planted firmly in the snow. Mandy lost her balance, and her body fell into Max's. He caught her in his arms, and held her to keep her from falling into the snow.

9

JAMES

Lying on his back in the snow, James took aim and squeezed the trigger. He got off two shots.

Another man fell.

But there was more shouting. More men. James didn't know how many, but there were a lot.

James scrambled to his feet, sprinting off again.

He didn't know in which direction he was headed in. All he knew was that he had to get out of there. He was outmanned and outgunned. Severely.

In the back of his mind, James knew he shouldn't get too far away from the camp. In this snow, it was likely he'd freeze to death before he found his way back again.

But that was only his second priority. His first was not getting shot.

So he ran, heading in a straight line. The visibility was so bad that trying to zig-zag didn't matter. He needed to put as much distance between himself and the enemy as possible.

It was hard to run in the snow, and he couldn't see where he was doing.

But he ran and ran. He was already out of breath. His heart was pounding. He clutched his gun in his hand. It seemed it was the only thing standing between him and death.

Who were these people? Were they from the compound?

More shouting.

It seemed as if two people appeared in front of him suddenly. Of course, it was just because of the bad visibility.

They shouted at him.

James's pulse was racing. Adrenaline coursed through him.

He raised his gun and pointed it at one of them.

How had they gotten in front of him? Had he accidentally run in a circle? Had he totally lost track of where he was?

The two figures in front of him had guns. But they didn't raise them.

They looked familiar. Somehow.

James's brain was a mess of chaos.

The two people were shouting at him. But he didn't seem to register the words.

Something held him back from shooting, from pulling the trigger. A small part of his brain seemed to be telling him to hold off.

But why?

He'd die if he didn't kill them first. He needed to shoot.

"James!" one of them was shouting.

The words of the two figures suddenly seemed to congeal. They suddenly started to make sense.

"James! It's me, John. Max's brother!"

"James! Come with us. What happened?"

James took a step closer, his gun still raised, his finger still on the trigger.

As he got closer, their faces came into better view.

Sure enough, it was John and Cynthia. The two newest members of the group.

There was no time to apologize for almost shooting them, though.

"Men with guns!" said James, not even able to catch his breath. He panted as he spoke the words.

"Where?"

"How many?"

"A lot. I shot one of them. No, two... Come on..."

"Camp's this way," said John, grabbing hold of James and pointing in a direction.

James peered in that direction, but he couldn't see anything except snow.

"He's badly shaken," Cynthia was saying to John. Her voice sounded distant and strange to James.

"James, can you make it back with us?"

James managed to nod.

Snow must have gotten inside his clothes and shoes when he'd tripped and fallen. He was really freezing now, his body trying to warm itself up by shaking violently.

Cynthia grabbed James's free hand, and started pulling him along.

"You two go first," shouted John, above the noise of the wind. "I'll follow."

"I can make it on my own," said James, pulling his hand away from Cynthia's grasp. "You might need to use your gun."

Cynthia nodded at him.

Cynthia led the way through the snow, her gun out and ready.

The three of them were weaving their way through the trees now. Mostly pines, completely covered in snow.

"You sure you know the way?" shouted James.

"John cut marks in the trees," shouted Cynthia.

Sure enough, there were gashes in the trees, creating a path that led back to camp. The gashes were large and once James spotted one of them, he couldn't stop seeing them.

"They'll lead the enemies right back to camp!"

"They're coming!" shouted John, from behind.

Cynthia and James spun around.

Sure enough, there was someone there. A tall figure, just his outline visible. Some sort of rifle in his hands. Just the outline of the rifle was visible.

James suspected it was a semi-automatic.

His mind seemed to be moving rapidly in a blur. Pure instinct took over.

James acted fast, before Cynthia did. He threw himself to the left, body-checking Cynthia with all his weight. They both fell to the ground.

John threw himself to the ground just in time.

The figure was firing. Bullets rained down around them, burying themselves into the snow.

John fired with his shotgun, from the ground.

The figure fell into the snow.

"Move!" shouted John, springing up from the ground.

Half of James's mind wanted to go retrieve the gun. But there would be more of them.

James got up, and dragged Cynthia up along with him.

John was already there, urging them forward. "Move!" he shouted again.

The snow was still blowing in powerful gusts that almost knocked them down.

The three of them dashed forward, away from the corpse in the snow, sprinting towards camp.

But camp wasn't going to be a safe haven. They'd been followed this far. There were more men out there. Heavily armed men. The slashes in the trees would lead them all right back to camp, right where James's mother and sister were.

They'd have to fight. Like they never had before.

10

GEORGIA

Georgia's back was stiff and painful. The cold weather was only making her injury worse. Still, she was getting stronger. She was much better off than she'd been a week ago.

She'd tried not to let it show, but she was worried about James. Very worried.

Despite the tough exterior she'd put on, Sadie saw right through it.

"He's going to be fine, Mom," said Sadie.

"I know," said Georgia.

She winced in pain as she stood there, the snow blowing around her.

"We've got to worry about ourselves right now," said Georgia. "We've got to be prepared for anything."

Georgia's mind was racing. At the camp, it was only herself, her daughter, and the two new members of the group, Jake and Rose.

It wasn't exactly the fighting force that Georgia would have liked it to be.

Sadie was getting more competent with her rifle.

But Jake and Rose were a completely different story. They'd never touched a gun in their lives. It boggled Georgia's mind that they'd been willing, before the EMP, to travel around the country in their van, without so much as a single handgun stashed safely away for self-defense.

Hopefully they'd change their tune soon. After all, while it may have been foolish to travel as they had without weapons in a pre-EMP world, it was downright suicidal to do so after the EMP. The world was different now, and Georgia doubted whether it would ever go back to how it had been before.

But so far, they hadn't shown much interest in learning about guns, even when Georgia had offered to show them when she'd been feeling energetic a few days ago.

Georgia wasn't feeling energetic now. She felt terrible. But she wasn't going to let that stop her.

"Get Jake and Rose," she said to Sadie, who nodded and dashed off through the snow.

Georgia stood there with her rifle, peering into the blank whiteness of nothing that swirled around her.

Suddenly, she heard something. Or thought she did.

But she couldn't see anything.

Then she heard it again.

Georgia got her rifle ready. Her finger was on the trigger. She positioned herself in the direction she thought the noise was coming from.

Nothing now. No noise.

Georgia glanced over her shoulder to see if Sadie had reappeared yet with Jake and Rose. No, she still wasn't there. What was taking so long?

Suddenly, figures burst out of the snow, coming into view.

Georgia recognized James immediately, despite the snow.

"James!" shouted Georgia.

She kept her gun up, though. She didn't immediately recognize the others. For all she knew, James was still in trouble. Just because he was back at camp didn't mean he was safe.

She pointed her rifle at them until she realized they were just John and Cynthia.

"Are you OK? What happened?"

Neither of the three of them looked injured, but it was hard to tell.

"They're following us," said James, completely out of breath, struggling to get the words out.

There wasn't any time to ask "who?"

"How many?" said Georgia, instinctively gripping her rifle tighter.

"We don't know," said John.

"Could be a lot," said James. "I shot two of them, I think. Can't remember. It happened so fast. And John. He got one."

"What were they armed with?"

"Semi-automatics."

"Do you think they can follow you back here?" said Georgia.

"Definitely," said Cynthia.

James and John nodded their agreement.

"Someone had the brilliant idea of making marks in the trees," said Cynthia. "Creating a trail that leads right back to our camp."

Georgia shot a glance at Cynthia. It seemed there was no end to her sarcastic witticisms, no matter how serious the situation.

At that moment, Sadie appeared through the snow, trailed by Jake and Rose.

"Oh no, are you all OK?" said Rose, shivering in the cold.

The wind was battering them all. They stood in at least a foot of snow. They couldn't even see the van or the tent. The camp was completely invisible to them, even though they were standing in the middle of it.

Jake and Rose weren't even carrying guns, even though there were plenty available for everyone now. The pot farmers had had plenty of guns. And there were enough bullets too. For the moment. They'd have to worry about their ammunition in the future. For now, it was survival. Immediate survival.

Max still wasn't back. Neither was Mandy. But she couldn't worry about them right now. They were on their own. There was nothing Georgia could do for them, or anything they could do for her. And no way to communicate.

Too bad those radios weren't really portable. It would have been invaluable to have an easily portable means of communication.

Georgia's mind was racing a mile a minute.

But this wasn't the time for musings.

Quick decisions needed to be made. Life or death decisions.

For all she knew, a horde of heavily armed men were about to burst into the camp.

"We need to get out of here," said James. "They're going to follow us right back here."

"But Max and Mandy won't know where we went," objected John.

"We can't worry about Max and Mandy right now,"

said Georgia. "But this is a good spot to defend from. There are trees all around us. We've got advantages if we stay here."

In the back of her mind, though, Georgia knew that the real reason she wanted to stay was so that Max and Mandy could find them again. After all they'd been through together, Georgia couldn't abandon them. Not like this.

Georgia's back was killing her, and she felt physically weak. She'd need to take that into account. She wasn't going to be able to rely on herself to step in when things got ugly. She'd have to count on herself possibility failing. If she didn't do that, everyone might die. Her kids might die.

"OK," said Georgia. "Jake and Rose, get a handgun each."

"But I don't even know how..."

"Get them!"

"We don't even know the first thing about..."

"Find the safety, switch it off. Point the gun, and pull the trigger." She spoke in a commanding way, daring them to challenge her. "Go!"

They rushed off into the snow, towards the van where the extra rifles were. There wasn't even time to be frustrated or furious with them.

"The rifles won't be of much use now," said Georgia. "since we can't see very far."

John, Cynthia, and James were still staring off into the direction they'd come from. But there was nothing. Nothing coming.

For now.

"We'll use the van," said Georgia. "We'll use it as a shield if we have too. Come on."

Georgia couldn't move that quickly through the snow with her injury. James held out his arm so she could use it as support, but she shook her head. "Keep your eyes peeled," she said. "Don't worry about me."

Georgia was wracking her brain for what kind of defense they could set up. Most of the ideas, though, would take a long time to set up. And the others, well, they weren't applicable in such heavy snow.

In the past, Georgia had relied on her rifles. She was a good shot at a distance. But that didn't matter now.

This was going to be close range fighting because of the visibility. But it was also out in the open. Completely different than an urban environment.

The trick, thought Georgia, was going to be create the kind of environment that they needed, the kind of environment in which they would have the advantage.

Georgia still had a few tricks up her sleeve.

11

ANTON

"They killed three of your men," said Marshal.

They were standing apart from the remaining men in a snowdrift, the snow practically up to their knees.

Anton was determined not to show weakness in front of Marshal or his men. He was determined to show nothing but victory. He was going to plow on ahead no matter what.

He'd destroy Max and the rest of them.

The idea of capturing the radios had become completely secondary to him.

"They didn't fight well," said Anton. "If they'd been better, they wouldn't have died."

"I don't know, man," said Marshal. "They did what they could."

"I thought you were tougher," said Anton.

"There's more to being tough than big words and a tough-guy attitude," said Marshal.

"What are you getting at?"

"I think this mission is a complete failure. We need to

turn around. Unless you want to lose the rest of your men."

"You're just worried about your own skin. You don't want to die out here in the snow."

"Look, man, I've been through worse. Much worse. I'm like a cockroach. Nothing can kill me."

Marshal's eyes stared right into Anton's. They seemed to penetrate him. They were dark and moody, intense and also horrible. Marshal saw something there that he hadn't seen before. After all, he wasn't in the habit of studying men's eyes. Or what they contained.

"You don't know what you're talking about," said Anton. "You're just scared."

"You can't trick me," said Marshal. "I'm not someone you can use petty little psychological tricks on to get what you want. I've been through the Army. Before prison. You didn't know that, did you? I've seen more combat than you'll ever see. I know how to survive, trust me. I'll do whatever it takes."

"You don't know shit," said Anton. "Anyone can say anything. There's no way to confirm that."

"Nope," said Marshal. "The EMP changed everything. We're just who we are now. No records. No nothing. You can think whatever you want of me. I don't give a shit. What I'm telling you is that if you continue, you're going to lose all your men, and probably your own life."

"You don't know what you're talking about." But the more Anton protested, the more he really did think that Marshal knew what he was talking about.

"It's your call, Anton," said Marshal. "It's your decision. If you want to attack, I'll be right there with you."

"But you'll ditch us at the last moment to save your own skin, right? Isn't that what you've been telling me?"

"You should know those of us who've been incarcerated take loyalty very seriously. I'm loyal to my old gang. And I'm loyal to the militia. I'm loyal to Kor. And my mission is to aid you. It's a matter of honor, of loyalty."

Anton eyed him, trying to see if he was telling the truth. He probably was. From the sound of it, those militia guys were crazy. Almost too intense.

"Hey, boss?" said one of the guys, calling out across the swirling snow. "What's the word?"

"You wait!" shouted Anton. "Until you hear otherwise, got it?"

"We're freezing our asses off, boss."

"Then light a fire or some shit," yelled Anton.

He thought being a leader was going to be easy. Kara had made the whole thing look like a cakewalk.

But here they were, his own men, questioning his orders.

It was enough to drive anyone insane.

He felt the anger rising through his chest, which felt as hot as a burning coal, despite the freezing wind.

He felt the anger in his head. His forehead was scorching hot.

"You get more respect from them talking to them… differently," said Marshal.

"I didn't ask for your opinion, OK?" snapped Anton.

"Whatever you say, Anton."

Anton stared at Marshal, quivering in anger.

But Marshal remained calm. Nothing seemed to shake him.

"Look," said Marshal. "I'm here as an envoy. Observe. But also help. Right?"

Anton just stared at him.

"What I'd do," said Marshal, "is I'd send in a scout. A single guy. See what's going on."

"But we know right where they are. The marks in the trees... they must lead back to the camp."

"Yes, but there's a reason you've been here stalling for an hour, right?"

Anton didn't say anything.

"Obviously the enemy knows how to fight. They know how to shoot. We can't underestimate them, and we've got to assume they're taking this time to set up some defenses."

"You don't think they'll just flee?"

"No, and neither do you. Or else you would have rushed in."

Anton knew he was right. Max and the others wouldn't want to abandon their gear. Their radios. Leaving their camp was as good as committing suicide. Anton knew that they didn't have proper winter gear. They didn't have it when they'd visited the compound, at least.

"Max is probably setting up some defenses," said Anton. "I don't think they'll flee. For a variety of reasons."

Marshal nodded. "I don't think they will, either. Now we've got to know what we're up against."

Anton nodded. The anger was starting to leave him. He was starting to see that Marshal was making some sense. Maybe Marshal really did want to help.

It had all gotten turned around in his head. It'd been the cold, the snow, the intense wind. He hadn't been expecting any of that.

Just a few hours ago, he'd been convinced he'd impress Marshal.

Now he wasn't sure what the roles were. It was all muddled.

Anton didn't like things like that. He liked things cut and dry. Clear. That was why he'd wanted to be the leader, to take power. If he ruled the compound, he could keep things simple. He could make things the way he liked them, and not have to worry about the wishes of others muddling things up for him. It'd be his way or no way.

"All right," said Anton. "I'll send someone in to see what they're up to. We'll be able to better coordinate our attack."

"All right," said Marshal, nodding. "Sounds like a good plan."

Anton shivered in the cold. His fingers and toes were freezing and going partially numb. He couldn't feel the end of his nose. There was ice building up on his eyelashes.

He'd never expected a storm to move in, nor for it to move in this fast. The dropping temperature was a surprise. Normally it dropped during the night, not during the day.

Marshal didn't seem affected by the cold. Maybe he was made of tougher stuff than Anton.

Anton was trying his best not to appear cold. But his body was shaking almost uncontrollably at this point.

He wasn't unusual. Marshal was the unusual one. If Anton was this cold, surely his men would be too.

If they were going to fight well, they'd need to warm up.

"OK," said Anton, clapping his numb hands together, and walking towards the men. "Ricky, you're going to be scouting."

"But, Anton..."

"I don't want to hear it, Ricky," said Anton, raising his hand. "Get in there close enough to see what's going on. Report back with information that'll help us attack."

Ricky stood there, his mouth hanging open. There was ice forming in his beard.

"You heard me," shouted Anton. "Now get going!"

Ricky stood frozen for a full ten seconds before he started to move.

Anton stared him down as he walked away, his eyes drilling holes into his snow-covered back.

Morale wasn't good. Anton could understand that. But he needed people to do what he said. He was the leader, after all.

"OK, you, over there."

"Wilson, sir."

"Wilson, yeah, get a fire started. The rest of you, help him get the wood."

"I don't know if we can start one in all this snow."

"I don't care how you do it. Just get it done."

Anton's voice was already feeling a little horse from yelling above the gusts of wind.

He walked back over to Marshal, who wasn't shivering.

A wry smile appeared on Marshal's lips. "You really told them, huh?"

"Maybe they're right," said Anton, ignoring him. "I don't know how they're going to get a fire started in this snow."

"If we don't, we're going to freeze to death. The sun's going to be going down soon."

"You don't sound worried about it. And why the hell are you smiling? You just said we might die."

"I'm just along for the ride," said Marshal, cryptically.

12

MANDY

Mandy couldn't feel her feet or her hands.

Max was in worse shape. And it wasn't a surprise. He was wearing the same jacket he'd been wearing all along. It wasn't designed for cold weather, and it was amazing he'd made it this far with the jacket.

Now he was paying the price.

Mandy didn't know if they'd make it back to camp before he froze to death.

"You've got to take my jacket, Max. Just for a little while."

Max shook his head.

"It's no longer a matter of being noble or whatever it is. You're being stubborn, and it's going to get you killed."

"I recognize that tree," said Max, through chattering teeth. "We're close by."

"And what if we're not? What if it's like the last three trees that I thought I recognized?"

"We'll have to make a fire," said Max. "It'll get us through the night."

Mandy wasn't so sure about that. For one thing, she didn't know if they'd be able to start a fire in the snow.

Maybe Max was right. Maybe this was time they finally found the camp. They'd been walking in circles for hours. Actual circles, not just that feeling when you're lost and you think you're walking in circles. They'd been intentionally walking in circles, hoping that they were close to the camp, and that they'd eventually stumble onto it.

For all Mandy knew, they could have passed twenty feet from the camp. They never would have known it.

Mandy trusted Max. He knew his limits. He was almost obscenely practical, even to the determinant of his own safety sometimes. But he'd always considered the safety of others. Especially Mandy. He'd never intentionally let his own stubbornness endanger her or the others.

But was Max fully aware of what he was doing? Had the cold affected him too much? Could she trust Max now? Was his judgment compromised?

Just when Mandy was thinking she might have to make some hard decisions, she saw something.

It was the unmistakable glowing light of a fire. It was roaring, a beacon of hope in the bitter harsh cold.

"Max," said Mandy, tugging on his arm. "Look!"

"Fire," muttered Max. "Fire..."

"Come on!"

"Could be a trap," said Max. He was starting to slur his words.

A figure appeared. Mandy didn't immediately recognize the silhouette.

Was Max right? Was it a trap?

The silhouette extended its arm. The light was lower

now, and visibility was worse than ever. The snow hadn't let up at all.

At the end of the silhouette's arm, there was the unmistakable outline of a handgun, backlit by the fire's flickering flames.

Someone shouted something.

Mandy raised her own gun.

She glanced at Max.

He had his gun raised too. But his hand was shaking badly. The cold was getting to him.

Was it possible they'd stumbled onto someone else's camp?

Then Mandy heard a familiar voice.

Georgia's. She was calling Mandy's name. And Max's.

The rest was a blur. Mandy remembered being taken by the fire to warm up, Max along with her. Blankets were draped over them. Someone took off Mandy's socks and examined her feet, checking for frostbite. Someone was doing the same for Max's.

As the minutes rolled by, Mandy was starting to warm up.

"What's the situation?" said Max.

"Just focus on warming up," said John, handing Mandy and Max each steaming cups of coffee.

"I'm fine," said Max. "But the enemy's out there. We can't let our guard down just because we're cold."

"No," said John. "We can't."

It was strange hearing the two of them talking. They had similar voices. It wasn't just their accents. It was something about their cadences, and the way they emphasized certain words. The main difference between their voices was that Max's was a little deeper, a little more serious.

John, on the other hand, sounded by comparison, at least, almost a little less severe.

"We've got three people officially on watch," said John. "But in reality, we're all on watch."

"This fire is going to just be announcing our presence," said Max.

"They already know where we are," said John. He started explaining what had happened, telling the story of the encounter he, James, and Cynthia had earlier.

"That doesn't make sense," said Max. "The guy we talked to from the compound said he was the scouting party. And you're saying there are how many men here?" Max briefly explained what had happened when he and Mandy had been out looking for the man who James had spotted yesterday.

"We don't know," said John. "But there are a lot."

"Maybe we should leave," said Mandy. The coffee was already making her feel warmer, and giving her that mental resilience that only caffeine could provide. "They know we're here. Did you stay here just because we were still out?"

John didn't answer.

"We can't leave," said Max. "Not with this snow. We won't make it."

"Are you sure?" said Mandy.

"It's time we made a stand," said Max. "We're not going to find anywhere better than here to live. If we can prove we can defend it, it'll be ours for the long haul."

"There are other places with deer," said Mandy. "Other places to find food."

"It's just rolling the dice," said Max. "And so far, every new place we've found has been worse than the last."

"That's not true. If we'd stayed at the farmhouse, we'd be dead by now."

"You know what I mean," said Max, standing up.

"Come on, Max," said John, moving over to his brother. "Stay by the fire. You've got to rest and warm up."

Max shook his head. "I'm fine," he said. "I'm plenty warm now. Now, let's see what you've got going for the defenses. The sun's almost down, and they'll probably attack after nightfall. We might not have very long."

"Georgia's figured everything out," said John.

"Where is she?"

"On the other side of the van."

The fire that Mandy sat near was up close against Jake and Rose's van. The van seemed to make the heat of the fire feel warmer, probably by reflecting the heat back towards her. Mandy made a mental note of that, in case it would be useful in the future. But then she realized they'd done it on purpose. Obviously she wasn't the first to take note of that useful trick.

Max glanced back once at Mandy before going around to the other side of the van, disappearing from view.

"Hell of a guy, eh?" said John to Mandy, who remained seated.

"He's done us a lot of good," said Mandy.

"I can see that. You all respect him a lot."

"We've got good reason too."

"Yeah," said John, letting his voice trail off vaguely.

"What's on your mind?" said Mandy, sensing that John wanted to say something, but wasn't sure if he should or not.

"Oh, nothing," said John.

"How'd you get this fire started?" said Mandy, eying the roaring fire.

"Lots of sap," said John. "It lights up like nothing else. And dead wood still on the trees. It's still dry, even in the snow."

Mandy nodded.

"I guess we could be attacked at any moment," said John, staring off into the swirling snow.

"Yup," said Mandy.

"I guess I've gotten kind of used to it," said John. "And you seem to have, too."

"What do you mean?"

"You're just sitting there, enjoying your coffee, rather than running around like a chicken with its head cut off."

Mandy shrugged. "I'm still so cold my limbs are almost too stiff to walk."

"That's not what I mean."

"I know what you mean. But I don't know. I guess you're right. I guess I've gotten used to it, too. And I trust Max."

"I can see that."

"Why do you say it like that?"

"Like what?"

"With that tone in your voice?"

"I don't know," said John. "You were asking what's on my mind. Well, I'll tell you. For weeks now, all I could think of was getting to Max. Finding Max. That's all Cynthia and I talked about. I thought Max would have all the answers. I figured Max would have everything set up perfectly at that farmhouse. And when he wasn't there, well, I guess it gave me something to keep going for."

"You thought Max would fix all your problems?"

"I guess so. He's my brother. I always looked up to him."

"That's not how he tells it."

"Yeah, well, we've had our differences. I went my own way for a while. I've changed since that. I mean, the EMP has changed all of us."

"So where are you going with all this?" said Mandy. "What's the point?"

She was thinking that one way the EMP might have changed her was she had less tolerance for emotional ramblings like the one John was launching into.

"I guess I'm just disappointed," said John. "I know I shouldn't be."

"You're disappointed Max doesn't have all the answers? Are you crazy? No one does. No one knows what happened. At least no one we're going to run into. And no one knows what the future holds. All we can do is try to live out the next day. And Max is good at that. We're getting good at it, too."

"I guess you're right," said John.

But Mandy was already feeling mad. No amount of backtracking on John's part was going to keep her from really letting him have it. Not at this point. She felt strongly about Max. Maybe she felt strongly for him.

"Now you listen here," said Mandy, raising her voice. She was mentally preparing the little speech she was going to give him. She was going to tell him he had no right to even start to criticize Max. She was going to tell him that...

There was a noise behind them.

"What's that?" said John, reaching for his handgun.

Mandy fumbled for her own gun. But her fingers were still stiff from the cold, and the gun seemed to be stuck in its holster.

13

RICKY

Ricky wasn't as scared of Anton as he was of Marshal.

But that didn't mean he didn't have to do what Anton said.

Ricky didn't know if Anton would take control of the compound like he wanted to. His intentions were clear, but would he have the ability to follow through?

Ricky doubted Anton would be a good leader. In fact, he knew otherwise. There were other men who were better suited to lead. There were more competent men. Men who knew what they were doing. But they weren't filled with the same intense lust for power that Anton exhibited.

Sometimes, all it took was the desire. The lust. Nothing more.

Provided he didn't die out here in the snow, Anton could easily take complete control of the compound.

And if that happened, Ricky didn't want to be on his shit list.

That'd mean a slow or quick death.

Anton could simply have him executed. Or he could start denying him food and other privileges. He could work him to death.

There were a thousand worse fates than a bullet in the back.

Violence was now the law of the land. Murders were the new normal. It wasn't like there was anyone who was going to start investigating murder cases.

It wasn't even called "murder" anymore. It was simply the way things were. The new reality.

People had already disappeared from the compound since Kara's disappearance. Some of them simply hadn't returned. Others had been called out to speak with Anton outside. They hadn't come back in. But Anton had.

Ricky was walking as slowly as possible through the trees. He followed the marks cut into the bark. Presumably they were leading him on a path back to Max's camp.

Ricky would have to think of a way to approach the camp without getting killed straight away. From what he'd heard, Max and his gang were extremely dangerous. Ricky didn't know if Max was former military or what. Maybe he was just a serious enthusiast, or had been before the EMP. After the EMP, he'd gone "professional," so to speak.

Sure, Max and his gang had fed the compound some sob story when they were there. But Ricky and the others weren't buying that now. Max and his gang had laid waste to the compound, killing many in the process of their daring escape.

Sure, if Ricky tried, he could almost see things from Max's perspective. Ricky and the others, led by Kara, had locked up Max's women. They'd wanted to keep them there for life. But they'd had good reasons. From one perspective, maybe Max had his reasons.

But Ricky wasn't the kind of person who liked to think about things from multiple perspectives. Life, after all, was easier when you looked at it just one way. From one angle. In black and white.

Ricky was using that same perspective now. The easiest thing for him to do was to follow orders. Not question them too much. Not think of the ways he was surely going to die. Not think of the ways he could fool Anton into thinking he'd scoped out Max's camp without actually doing so. And not simply escaping on his own.

After all, if Ricky ran off, intent on saving his own hide, what terrible end would he meet? It'd probably be sooner rather than later. That much was sure. He wouldn't be able to feed himself, for one thing. Most likely though, was the possibility that he'd simply be killed by some roving band.

Led by Anton and Marshal, Ricky and the other men from the compound had already come across one such band on their way here to find Max. There'd been a brief gunfight. None of the compound men took any fire. But they easily could have.

There'd just been three of the others. Armed with one shotgun and two machetes, they'd been no match for Ricky and the others.

But if Ricky had been on his own, it would have gone much differently.

The EMP had changed everyone. It seemed as if the only ones who had survived the initial panic were the most vicious, the most cruel, and the most willing to do whatever it took.

There were some, like Max and his gang, who claimed to follow the "rules," whatever those were, as if they were guided by some principles.

But Ricky knew differently. There was no right or wrong any more. It was simply kill or be killed.

And they'd all die sooner or later.

Ricky had no illusions that any of them would last another five years. Not with the way things were going.

The temperature had dropped further now that it was night. Ricky shivered in the cold, despite his huge, warm parka.

The snow had stopped falling. The wind had died down.

The moon had risen. It was high and large in the sky, casting light that the fallen snow reflected brilliantly. There was no need for a flashlight.

Up ahead, Ricky could see the flickering flames of a fire reflecting off the snow.

He stopped, staying completely still. He didn't hear anything. But there were definitely people at the camp. Max was still there.

Why hadn't they left? They must have known they'd be followed.

Maybe the fire was a decoy. Or some kind of diversion.

Max was smart. Ricky knew that much. You didn't fight your way out of the compound and not have some kind of practical intelligence.

Max wouldn't want to sit there like a sitting duck with a raging fire. Or would he?

Ricky didn't know what the status of the men at the camp was. Maybe they were injured. Maybe they were half-starving. Maybe some of them were dying from the cold.

Despite his initial trepidation, Ricky found his mindset shifting.

Maybe Ricky was just trying to convince himself to go

ahead, to get close enough to the camp to scout it. After all, he knew that if he didn't come back with relevant information, it was likely that he'd simply be executed. Or punished in some other horrible way.

Ricky had seen a movie once in which a World War II soldier had been punished by being chained to a huge boulder. The soldier had been Dutch, maybe. Or maybe Swedish. Ricky couldn't remember now. And it was likely that that movie would never be seen by anyone ever again. So it didn't matter.

The soldier had been left there to die, to starve to death and be picked apart by wild animals.

Ricky could easily imagine something like that happening to himself. Anton was obviously eager to show he was a tough leader. He wouldn't hesitate to make an example out of someone who didn't do what he was supposed to do.

Only in Ricky's case, unlike in the movie, he'd probably die from the cold before he died of starvation.

So was Ricky trying to get himself to do his job, to continue towards the camp and gather real information?

Maybe.

And he was aware of it.

In the end, he decided to just go on ahead. After all, the chances of everyone at the camps being in good fighting condition, in good health, was very low.

Conditions couldn't have been harsher. Food couldn't have been scarcer.

Probably, Max and the others were barely hanging on by a thread.

Ricky could probably take them all out by himself. If he wanted to.

And maybe he did.

After all, what would impress Anton more than coming back with the news that he'd singlehandedly killed them all? That he'd recovered the radios by himself?

Ricky and Ricky alone would have saved the day. He would have avoided the possibility that the others of his party would be injured in a fight. He would have saved them all the trouble... of everything.

Ricky could feel his heart accelerating as he mentally prepared himself for going in there on his own and killing Max and the others. He didn't know how many there were. But he had a rough idea. Probably about the same number as had been in the compound. Unless some of them had died off like flies in the winter.

He probably shouldn't go, though.

It was stupid, right?

Then again, his other option was simply to return to Anton and Marshal and the rest. Ricky knew he was on the shit list for one reason or another. Anton had chosen him, after all, and not the others, for this dangerous task. He was disposable in Anton's mind. Sooner or later, Anton might find a reason to have him die.

But if he returned completely victorious, having gone above and beyond, Ricky wouldn't be on the shit list anymore.

And if he died by barging into the camp all by himself, then so what?

He was feeling nihilistic. He'd die soon enough, anyway. Better to go out with a bang than flounder around in the freezing snow, waiting for Anton's mood to shift for the worse.

Ricky decided it was time. Finally.

He'd approach the camp from the other side, where

the light of the fire didn't reach. He'd approach from the darkest corner, slinking along in the night where the tall snow covered trees shielded the ground from the bright light of the moon.

He'd do what he had to do.

Or what he thought he had to do.

Everyone's path was different. It'd always been like that. But since the EMP, each path had become more intense. More perilous.

That was just the way it was.

14

JAKE

"I feel like I'm losing it," whispered Jake to Rose.

They were cuddled in the honeymoon position in their van.

Everyone else was outside by the fire, keeping watch, keeping warm, and staying ready. An attack was expected at any moment.

Jake and Rose had probably annoyed everyone else by saying they'd needed to rest in the van. Max had just scowled and told them they had five minutes to themselves, and that after that he wanted them back out there.

Jake had said they'd had something very personal to discuss. Something that was at the crisis level. Something that didn't affect the rest of them. Only Jake and Rose.

Max had been a tough sell. He hadn't wanted to let anyone out of his sight. But Jake had convinced him. Max and the others probably thought Rose was pregnant or something, the way Jake had talked.

In reality, Jake was suffering another one of his bouts of intense anxiety. Severe panic. He'd felt it coming on, and knew he'd needed to get away from everyone. Rose was the only one he could be around, the only one he felt comfortable with.

He'd always been an anxious person. Through high school, he'd always hung in the back of the bus, of the classroom. He'd always been the one against the wall at the school dances, never participating, but somehow feeling like he was accomplishing something by just being there.

It'd gotten a little worse in college. He'd spent all his time alone in his dorm room. When it'd been time to go to the dining hall to eat, his heart would start to pound and he'd start to sweat bullets. A lot of nights, he'd just sit there, crouched in a corner of his dorm room, never leaving to eat.

He'd gone hungry more nights than he could count. And that's when he'd realized that his general anxiety had turned into something worse. Much worse.

Somehow he'd graduated college. And with high grades in all subjects. He'd made the dean's list almost every semester. Isolating himself in his room had given him almost nothing to do but study.

After college, he'd met Rose.

She'd changed everything.

The anxiety had started to melt away. Soon enough, he was going out with her. To parties, to dinners with friends. All the things he'd always wanted to do but had been too scared to.

She'd completely changed him. And it wasn't anything specific she'd done. It was just her presence. And how much he was in love with her.

With Rose, the anxiety and panic attacks felt like distant memories. He almost couldn't remember what the feeling had been like.

They'd become digital nomads, deciding to travel the country in their van.

Even after the EMP, the anxiety and panic attacks had stayed away. Jake had even lasted through the torments of the pot farmers.

But now...

It was all too much.

The panic attacks had apparently come back.

"It's going to be OK, Jake," said Rose, speaking to him in a soothing voice.

"Nothing's OK," said Jake.

His skin was sweaty and cold at the same time. His heart rate was extremely elevated.

It didn't feel like he could catch his breath.

"I can't breathe," said Jake, pushing away from Rose.

He needed air. He couldn't breathe. Not with her next to him.

And not in the van.

"I've got to get out of here," said Jake.

"Jake!" said Rose, grabbing his arm. "It's all going to be OK. You just need to wait this out. We can stay in here, in the van. It's just the two of us. You don't need to worry about anyone else."

But Jake knew that wasn't true.

He did have to worry about everyone else. He had to worry about it all. Everything.

There were men with guns. Coming to kill them.

But it wasn't even that fact that was getting to him.

He didn't even know what it was.

It was just this overwhelming feeling of dread. Of complete panic. And that was slowly morphing into the feeling of being trapped.

Completely trapped. Suffocating.

"I'll be right back," said Jake, tugging his arm away from Rose's grasp.

He opened the door to the van. Cold air rushed in.

Not far away, there were the others. Some were huddled around the fire. Others were staring off into the night.

He could see everything. The moon was bright. And that meant everyone could see him. There was nowhere to hide.

He needed a dark corner. Like the van.

But then he couldn't breathe.

His mind was running circles. Nothing but pointless circles.

And he didn't realize it. He was losing control of himself.

"You OK, buddy?" said John.

He seemed to have come out of nowhere. He stood there, in front of Jake, with a huge gun in his hands.

Jake couldn't find the words. He couldn't answer. He was breathing too hard.

"I think he's having a panic attack," said Rose, from somewhere behind him.

"Come on, buddy," said John, attempting to put his arm around Jake. "It's going to be OK."

"Get off me!" shouted Jake, twisting away from John.

He needed to get away. He needed to breathe.

Even Rose couldn't calm him down this time.

"Jake!" shouted Rose.

But it was too late.

He was off, running away from the camp as fast as he could.

He had nothing with him but the clothes on his back.

There was shouting behind him, but he couldn't make out the words. He ignored it.

He felt like a cornered animal.

Jake ran across the snow, through the moonlight.

It felt good to run. It was better out here, away from everyone.

The cool air felt good in his lungs. Soothing.

Jake ran and ran. He was far away from the camp now. The only thing he could hear was the sound of his boots hitting the ground as he kicked up snow.

Exhausted from running, he slumped down, his back against a tree. The seat of his jeans rested in the snow. It was cold, but he didn't care.

He looked out into nature. It was beautiful, the freshly fallen snow covering the trees like blankets. Scenes like this were why he and Rose had wanted to travel the country. They'd wanted to take it all in. They'd wanted to experience nature rather than living out their lives locked away in some office building under fluorescent lighting.

Minutes ticked by, and Jake was unaware of them. A few minutes turned into half an hour. Then an hour.

Out here, his mind was starting to feel clearer.

He was physically exhausted from the running. He didn't know how far he'd gone, but when he turned to look, he couldn't see any hint of the camp or the campfire.

Jake put his fingers to his neck, to check his pulse. It was still beating rapidly. But that was normal from the running. He wasn't going as fast as when he'd had the panic attacks.

Had he gotten over it?

The freezing temperatures felt good. They seemed to sap the heat and anxiety from his body.

Jake stood up, dusting himself off.

He was ready to return to camp. He'd have to apologize to Rose. She'd understand, though. He'd told her all about the panic attacks he'd used to have. The others, though, might not be so understanding.

He had, after all, put everyone in danger. Maybe they'd come out looking for him, exposing themselves to the enemies who could strike the camp at any moment.

"Who are you?"

The voice was unfamiliar. It was coming from behind him.

Jake turned to look.

A wild-looking man was standing there. His hair was long and greasy. His beard was scraggly and wild.

He wore a huge parka. He held some kind of rifle in both hands. It was pointed right at Jake.

Jake didn't have a gun with him. The others at camp had made him take one, but he must have left in the van. During the panic attack, carrying a gun had been the last thing on his mind.

Not that he had any idea how to use it anyway.

Jake's heart started beating faster.

He might have been about to have another panic attack.

But it probably didn't matter.

It was too late.

15

ANTON

"Ricky's not back yet?" said Anton.

The man shook his head.

Anton couldn't remember his name. To Anton, he was just another lackey. Nothing but a soldier. Someone who would do his bidding. Someone who would raise Anton to greatness. He wasn't one of the important ones. Not someone he was trying to impress.

Not like Marshal.

"What's the word?" said Marshal.

"Seems like Ricky's not back," said Anton.

The men were sitting around the fire. They'd been there for what felt like hours.

At this point, they were once again warm. Not to mention well fed.

They'd bought plenty of good food with them, and Anton could tell the men were feeling better.

This was the rest they'd needed.

The snow had stopped falling, and the night seemed peaceful and calm. If it hadn't been for the reality of the mission and the EMP, they could have been mistaken for a group of very committed hunters.

Not that their weapons would have been typically used by hunters.

Anton, though, wasn't as relaxed as the rest of the men. The pressure to impress Marshal was growing on him. He needed to get this over with. And the sooner the better.

Anton glanced over at Marshal, who seemed as calm as ever.

"All right," said Anton. "We're going to move on out. It's time."

"What about the scout? Ricky?" said Marshal.

"What about him?"

"I thought the plan was to wait until he got back."

"It was," said Anton, inflating his chest instinctively, even though it wasn't visible underneath his parka. "But apparently he's not coming back. Maybe he ran off. He was always a coward. Or maybe he got killed. We don't have anything to worry about, anyway."

"I don't know," said Marshal. "I thought this Max figure was supposed to be clever. And dangerous."

"What do you care? I thought you said you were just along for the ride?"

Marshal shrugged and gave Anton one of his perplexing half-smiles. It unnerved Anton, right down to his bones. But he chose to ignore it.

"I'm in charge," said Anton. "These are my men, and I'm saying we go."

"Your call," said Marshal, seeming not to care too much either way.

Anton gave the order, and the men started packing up their gear, checking their weapons. The mood was jovial.

They'd eaten, and spirits all around were better. The men joked with each other as they got ready.

"We're going to slaughter them."

"They won't know what hit them."

"Max is as good as dead."

"I'm going to be the one who gets him."

"Says who?"

"Yeah, says who? He's fair game to all of us."

"No, he's mine."

"That's what you think."

"He killed my brother."

"At the compound?"

"Shit, man, I didn't realize."

"He's still fair game."

"Come on, you better let Art have him. He killed his brother, man."

"He killed a lot of people."

The banter was getting Anton feeling better about it all. They would, after all, completely slaughter Max and his group.

Max, for all of his apparent cunning, didn't stand a chance.

Anton's group were committed men. Basically soldiers. They were well fed, well-rested, and better armed.

Sure, they'd had to walk a long way to get here. But for all the past weeks and months, they'd slept on their bunks in the compound. Max's group, on the other hand, had been living like animals, sleeping where they could, struggling to eat, struggling to survive.

Anton's men were strong. They'd take them easily.

"All right, men," said Anton, addressing the group.

The banter died down.

Anton tried to make his voice deep and commanding-sounding.

"We'll break into two groups," said Anton. "You three, come with me. We'll approach from the north. The rest of you, you'll go with Marshal. You'll hit them from the east."

Marshal glanced at Anton.

"That OK with you, Marshal? You leading one of the groups."

"Fine by me," said Marshal. That strange smile was still on his lips. It worried Anton. Was Marshal up to something? He tried to push the thought to the back of his mind.

"We'll all head there together," said Anton. "Once we get in sight of the camp, we'll break up into our two groups. We won't have to worry about crossfire if we stay strict with our approach angles. So use your compasses. Visibility's good, so we won't have to worry about that. We've got the advantage of better firepower. We'll hang back and pump them full of bullets."

"We can't lose!"

"They won't know what hit them."

Anton smiled wryly at the men. They were obviously ready for victory.

There was no way they could lose.

Max didn't stand a chance.

16

MAX

Despite the dropping temperatures, Max was warmer now. The fire had helped immensely. He would have been dead without it. His body was still stiff, and didn't feel quite right.

He'd gotten too cold. He'd let his mind start to slip away. He and Mandy could have easily died out there, lost in the snow, not to be found until the following day.

Max hadn't seen Jake dash off into the woods.

But he'd learned about it soon enough. John had rushed over to tell him.

"Problems with Rose and Jake," he'd said.

"What happened?" said Max, turning his attention away from the surrounding woods.

"Jake ran off. Panic attack. Rose ran after him."

Max didn't know what to do. He had to make a decision quickly.

At any moment, the enemy could attack. And Max was expecting the worst. Expecting that it'd be more men than they were counting on. That they'd have better guns than they were expecting. And that they were more strategically-minded and ruthless.

If they went after Rose and Jake, they'd risk leaving the camp less defended than it should have been. Even if they only sent one or two people. And it wasn't something that Max could tell someone else to do. It'd have to be him.

If he left, that meant leaving the camp and his friends. It'd be as bad as leaving Jake and Rose out there alone.

After all, the longer Jake and Rose stayed away from the camp, the more likely they were to die.

"Are they armed?"

"I think Rose is. But Jake isn't."

"Shit," muttered Max.

"Should we go after them?"

Max was thinking as fast as he could.

It was one of the tough decisions. But they all tended to be that way. And there was a limit to how used to it you could get.

Max shook his head. "No," he said. "We can't risk leaving the camp less defended than it is."

"But they'll die out there," said John.

Max nodded. "Maybe."

"You can't just let them die."

"We need to stay here," said Max.

"We've got to go," said John. "We can't leave them out there on their own."

John's face was starting to show his anger and frustration.

Since meeting his brother again, Max had been impressed with how practical John had gotten. He was a different man than the one Max remembered from before the EMP. The events had changed him. His new life had changed him.

So it surprised Max that John wanted to risk all their lives for Jake and Rose. After all, Jake and Rose hadn't been too keen to carry guns, to learn how to use them, or to learn any number of things that would have saved their own lives.

Everyone needed to be responsible for their own safety. To an extent. Those who weren't, well, that was the breaks.

And John knew that. And Max knew that John knew that.

There was something else going on. There was some kind of frustration that John was carrying inside him. And it didn't have to do with Jake and Rose. It had to do with Max.

Max knew what it probably was. John had thought Max had had all the answers. He thought that Max would save him.

And now that he'd found Max, the reality was tough to swallow. Sure, Max sometimes knew what he was doing. He was good at certain things. But he hadn't been in the military. He wasn't an expert fighter. He was a practical man who knew his own limitations. He thought clearly in desperate situations. He had a good head on his shoulders, and the ability to keep pushing on and on when the going seemed impossible.

But that wasn't enough for John. He'd wanted a savior. Someone who wasn't even human. Someone who could save not only John, but Jake and Rose too.

Maybe in John's mind the fact that Max was "giving up," on Jake and Rose meant that he'd give up on John at some point too.

And that wasn't who Max was. He wasn't a savior. He'd

tried to save Chad. He'd done all he could, and Chad had died anyway. It'd been Chad's own fault.

"John," said Max, quietly. "Leave them. Hopefully they'll come back."

John didn't say anything. His eyes gleamed with something that wasn't quite anger. But it was as intense as anger.

There wasn't time to worry about all that, though. Max knew it was only a matter of time before the enemy would arrive. This wasn't the time to hash out some kind of strange sibling rivalry. Or whatever it was.

"I'm going to check on James," said Max.

John nodded but said nothing.

Max left him, and began trudging through the snow towards the spot where James was hidden.

As soon as Max had been able to think clearly again after almost freezing to death, he'd come up with the idea of positioning three scouts around the camp.

Currently, James, Sadie, and Cynthia were in three separate locations, hidden in the snow and the trees. Each of their positions was a few hundred feet away from camp. If one looked at it from a bird's eye view, the three points formed a triangle that surrounded the camp. That gave them complete visibility for anyone approaching.

James, Sadie, and Cynthia were chosen because they were some of the physically smallest members of the group. And they all had experience, too. Max had known he could count on them, whereas Jake and Rose were still a completely unknown quantity.

And it was good he hadn't decided to count on them. They'd rushed off into the woods, probably to meet their own demise.

Max couldn't think about them now.

Mandy, of course, had volunteered in Cynthia's place, but she'd been still recovering from almost freezing to death. She'd needed time by the fire. If the enemy didn't show up for hours, there was always the possibility of rotating the watch. But for now, Max had wanted those three out there.

The plan was that if James, Sadie, or Cynthia spotted anyone approaching, they were to dash back to the camp and warn the others.

The only problem with the plan was that the temperature had dropped, and the three wouldn't have the warmth of the fire.

But Max had packed them all in with a good amount of snow, which would actually act as an insulator, helping to keep them warm.

He was headed now to check on each one of them, to make sure they hadn't gotten too cold.

But before Max had reached the edge of camp, before he'd even gotten to the tree line, he heard footsteps pounding heavily on the ground.

Max's hand was already on his Glock. He had it drawn and ready, finger on the trigger.

He saw movement in the trees. Someone was sprinting at top speed right towards him.

He saw the face, and it took him a moment to recognize who it was.

It was James, his gun in his hands, terror on his face.

"They're coming!" He spoke in a hushed whisper, but the urgency was clearly there in his voice.

"How many?"

"Three or four. I'm not sure."

"Come on."

Max turned on his heel and dashed back to the fire,

where the others were. He could hear James running behind him.

So far, Max's plan had worked. They had advance warning.

But they'd need more than just that to survive.

If they stayed in the camp, they'd be sitting ducks.

The van probably wouldn't work as any kind of permanent shelter, except to obscure them briefly from view. The bullets would pierce the metal. The van wouldn't keep them safe.

To stay alive, they'd need to snap into action. They'd need to execute the second part of Max's plan.

Max reached the fire only seconds before James.

James put his hands on his knees, doubling over, his breathing fast and rapid from sprinting.

"They're coming," said Max. "James saw them."

The heads turned towards him. Terror colored their faces.

But they weren't the types to let fear destroy them, to let it paralyze them. They were strong, and Max's attitude had rubbed off on all of them.

They grabbed their guns, standing up rapidly.

They knew the plan. But they looked to Max for further instruction.

"We need to get the other scouts," said Max. "Mandy, you know where Sadie and Cynthia are. Bring them to the place we talked about. We'll meet you there."

Mandy nodded.

Suddenly, the sound of footsteps thundering through the snow hit Max's ears.

He turned to look, his Glock still ready.

"It's Sadie!"

Sadie was running top speed towards them, her fairly

short arms and legs pumping with incredible speed.

"They're coming!"

"Shit," muttered John.

"Two groups?" said Mandy.

Georgia said nothing. There was only grim determination on her face.

Max hadn't been expecting that the enemy would split up like that. He'd been expecting only one single scout to come rushing back.

Despite the surprise, there was nothing to do but act.

And fast.

"Mandy," said Max, pointing to the area where Cynthia lay in hiding, waiting and watching.

The possibility of three groups was unlikely. And if they had splintered into three groups, it didn't matter. The strategy at this point was going to be the same.

They were coming from the north and the east.

Max's plan had been to have everyone at camp sneak away, hiding within the trees in locations where they'd be able to attack the enemy. The unexpected locations would be their advantage, along with the thick cover of the trees. The enemy would come in, expecting an easy battle, expecting to simply pepper the camp with bullets, slaughtering everyone there.

Max was playing the guerrilla warfare game. He'd scouted the area, and already shown everyone where they were to hide. They'd be spread out, and the enemy would hopefully be clustered together.

But the enemy had thrown a wrench in Max's plans.

He'd had no provisions for a situation like this, with two approaching enemy groups.

There wasn't time to curse himself. He'd have to improvise.

Mandy was already rushing off to Cynthia.

Max glanced at Georgia, Sadie, John, and James. They were watching him expectedly, thinking he had the answer.

Hopefully he did.

Should they flee?

There weren't many of them. They could dash off into the woods. Maybe they could escape. Maybe they could make it.

John, seeming to read Max's thoughts, spoke up. "We should flee," he said. "We don't have a chance."

Hearing it spoken out loud helped Max make up his mind. "No," he said. "This camp is ours. We're defending it."

Without their supplies, without their food, they'd be as good as dead in a few days' time if they fled.

"They won't let us live," said Max. "They'll hunt us down. We'll be half-frozen, and they'll kill us easily if we leave."

Mandy and Cynthia arrived, panting with exertion.

There wasn't much time.

"Mandy, you and James are coming with me. Georgia, you've got John, Cynthia, and Sadie. I'll hit the old territory. Georgia, get into position over in that direction to take on the eastbound group." Max pointed to a part of the forest where Georgia would have a good shot at the group coming from the east. "Cynthia and John, carry Georgia if she can't make it. OK, let's move! There's not much time."

There was no more time for talking. The atmosphere was tense, but not frantic. Everyone was in action. Everyone was on the move.

Max glanced behind him. Georgia was limping behind

John, Cynthia, and Sadie. A moment later, John and Cynthia stopped, and got on either side of Georgia.

Max turned his head. The others, unfortunately, were on their own for now. He couldn't worry about them, or about Georgia's injury.

They didn't have much time to get to their positions.

The clock was ticking.

17

RICKY

As Ricky had gotten closer to the camp, he'd quickly chickened out and completely abandoned his plans to take on everyone by himself. He'd retreated back into the woods, wondering what to do.

That was when he'd come across one of them. He was tall and fairly young, completely out of breath, and apparently completely unarmed. There was a wild look on his face and in his eyes. Ricky didn't know what to make of him. The only thing Ricky knew was that this was the opportunity he'd been looking for, the opportunity that would save him.

All Ricky needed was information.

But the man wasn't talking.

"Who are you?" repeated Ricky.

The man stared back at him with his wild eyes. Ricky couldn't look too long at those eyes. There was something about them that unnerved him.

"Speak!" shouted Ricky.

He was losing his patience. He didn't have all night,

after all. He'd been gone a long time. He needed to get back to Anton with the information.

The man opened his mouth, but no sound came out.

"What the hell is wrong with you?" shouted Ricky. "You want something to make you talk? Well, I'll give you something."

Ricky had his pistol out and in his hand. He took reckless aim, and squeezed the trigger. The gun's recoil was satisfying. As was the sound. He'd been lucky enough to get a high caliber pistol. He liked the seriousness of the weapon, the way it made an impact.

The bullet struck the man in the knee. He screamed in pain, clutched his knee, tried to maintain his balance on one leg, and then fell down into the snow.

Ricky walked slowly over to him, his rifle slung across his back, his pistol pointed at the man's head.

"You've got to know that you're going to leave this world soon enough, buddy. You might as well make it easier on yourself. I've got five more bullets right here loaded, and plenty more in my pocket."

"Don't..." muttered the man, wincing from the pain.

"Don't what? Come on," said Ricky. "Don't hate me. This is nothing personal. I'm probably in a worse situation than you. I've got an asshole boss who's been breathing down my neck. That's bad enough, but you know how it is since the EMP. Now it's life and death, even if it's just a bad boss. Same shit as before, only magnified."

"I don't know what you're talking about."

"Pity you're wasting your dying breath with words like that," said Ricky.

Ricky stood over the man, one leg on either side of his body. Ricky pointed his revolver straight down at the man's head.

Standing there, having shot the man in the knee, Ricky knew that he had the power of life and death in his hands. And if made him feel good. He felt powerful. When he'd been with the other men from the compound, he'd felt weak. At any moment, an order from Anton could see him executed. Or worse.

Now it was Ricky who was in charge.

Practical thoughts soon flew out the window. Ricky momentarily forgot what he was trying to do. He didn't remember that he was trying to get information that would keep him alive, keep Anton from murdering him out of frustration.

The sense of power over this man had completely overwhelmed him.

"We're all in this shit world together now," said Ricky. "Although this new world isn't exactly a team sport, if you know what I mean. It's every man for himself. And sooner or later, it's all going to get us. The grim reaper, the big man with the scythe, whatever you want to call him."

Ricky was getting carried away with himself, ranting like there was no tomorrow. He recognized somewhat that he was losing control, but he let himself continue. It was fun, after all, to be in power, to wield life and death, to speak with authority.

"OK," said Ricky. "I'm going to give you something else to think about. And after that, we'll see how much you want to tell me. I have a feeling that you're not as tough and silent as you'd like to think you are."

Ricky aimed the pistol at the man's shoulder. He squeezed the trigger.

The man screamed, his face contorting in agony.

Ricky had always thought that the knee was one of the most painful places to get shot, but the shoulder seemed to really do it this time. Ricky briefly wondered why. Did the man have an old injury? Was the whole "shot in the knee" myth just that, a myth? Or was it simply that two injuries hurt more than one alone?

Suddenly, for a brief moment, the expression of pain on the man's face vanished. His eyes darted to the side, seemed to show some recognition, and then came immediately back to Ricky's gun, where they'd been pointed before.

"You see something out there, buddy?" said Ricky, turning his head in the direction that Ricky had looked.

Ricky didn't see anything. It was just the same old regular snow-covered woods.

But he'd sworn that the man had seen something. Something familiar, something that would make him momentarily forget the intense pain of two gunshot wounds.

"Who's out there?" said Ricky, his voice becoming tense and agitated. His mood was starting to shift again, this time to paranoia.

The man's eyes flickered off to the side once more.

Ricky turned again to look.

But it was too late.

Something heavy hit Ricky in the back of the head. Hard.

Pain seared through his skull. It felt like someone had driven a steel spike through the back of his skull.

He reeled in pain, falling to the ground. The cold snow covered his face, somehow making the pain even worse.

18

ROSE

Rose had gotten there too late. She'd been all over in search of Jake.

When she'd finally found him, he'd already been shot.

She hadn't brought a gun with her. She'd been too frantic and too concerned about Jake to remember a firearm. The whole world of guns was completely foreign to her. It always had been. Even over the last day, with the imminent threat of an attack, guns were still the last thing on Rose's mind.

And she was regretting that attitude now.

She was panicking. There wasn't anything she could do.

But she had to do something.

Rose had hidden behind a tree, peeking her head out. When she'd been trying to figure out what to do, half-paralyzed by fear and panic, she'd seen the stranger shoot Jake again.

Jake was still alive.

He could be saved.

She'd finally acted.

The stranger had been distracted by his own semi-coherent ramblings. Rose had dug through the snow until she'd found a heavy stick. A good, heavy one. Plenty of heft to it.

Rose held the branch high above her, then swung it down as hard as she could. She heard and felt the heavy wood connecting with the man's skull.

The stranger fell heavily onto the snow with a grunt of pain. Half his body had fallen on top of Jake.

"Jake! Are you OK?"

Rose bent down, frantically trying to push the stranger's body off of Jake. The stranger wasn't moving. He was heavy, but she managed to push him completely off of Jake.

Jake didn't look good. The color was draining quickly from his face. His eyes were half-closed. He'd been shot twice, once in the shoulder and once in the knee. Blood had soaked through his jacket at the shoulder.

"Rose..." said Jake, his voice sounding like it was fading away.

"It's OK, Jake," said Rose. She was trying to make her voice not sound as frantic as she felt. A single tear rolled down her cheek. "It's going to be OK, Jake."

"We should have..."

"What is it, Jake?"

Rose felt completely overwhelmed. She couldn't do this. She didn't have it in her to watch the only man she'd ever loved die before her eyes. She tried to remember something about first aid. Shouldn't she make a tourniquet, or do something to stop the bleeding?

She didn't know.

She stared down at Jake's face that was so full of pain

she could barely stand to look at it, not having the slightest idea what she should do next. She was letting the panic overwhelmed her and take control of her completely.

Rose's leg was pushed up against the stranger. He still hadn't moved, but she didn't know if he was dead. She hadn't checked his pulse, or even looked at his face since he'd hit him.

Rose's heavy stick lay on the ground, half buried in the snow, completely forgotten.

The stranger's leg suddenly moved. Rose felt it against her.

She spun her head to look at him.

Just at that moment, the stranger made his move.

He'd either been lying in wait, waiting to make his move, or he'd just woken up out of his daze.

He moved fast, scrambling into position, and then lunging up from the snow at Rose.

His body hit hers heavily. He knocked her onto her back. Her head hit the ground hard, her neck snapping back. Snow kicked up into the air around them.

The stranger's face was right against hers. He kept her pinned down with one arm. She thrashed at him, scratching his face with her nails, drawing blood.

But he just grinned down at her.

She couldn't get out from under his weight.

But it'd be OK.

Jake would save her. He was so close by. He was right there. He'd always been there for her before.

It'd only be a few more seconds. Just a matter of time.

"Jake!" cried Rose.

The stranger was reaching for something in the snow. His eyes didn't leave Rose's as he fumbled in the snow with his free hand, searching for something. Probably his gun.

"Jake!"

But there was no answer from Jake.

What was he doing?

"Ah, there we go. Found it," muttered the stranger, leering down at Rose with intense eyes full of anger. "This is a new world now, lady, and you've got to learn to finish what you start. You don't bash someone in the head like that and not finish the job. 'Cause they're going to come back for you."

"Jake!" cried out Rose. There was an intense desperation in her voice. She'd never even heard herself use that tone before. She felt more hopeless than she'd ever felt.

Sure, she'd encountered problems in the past. Life before the EMP hadn't been easy for her, in comparison to her friends. But those problems were nothing in comparison to the problems of her new life.

And now she'd finally encountered the worst problem of all. The one she'd never survive.

"I'm going to enjoy this," snarled the stranger. With his thumb, he pulled back the hammer of his gun. "More than anything, I'm doing you a favor."

"Please," cried Rose. "Please don't."

If she could buy more time, Jake would save her. He was gravely injured, but surely he'd manage to marshal his strength to save the love of his life.

"Too late, lady."

The stranger seemed to be enjoying this. That was good. All she need was more time, and the stranger seemed willing to give it to her.

"I don't deserve this," cried Rose.

"We deserve everything we get. It's all coming to us, whether we like it or not."

Was Rose going to leave the world believing that someone else would step in and save her?

Finally, something clicked in her mind.

Her survival instincts kicked in.

Strong instincts.

No one else was going to help her.

Jake wasn't going to.

No one was.

Only she could do it.

Rose let out a furious scream and pushed herself up against the man, using all her strength and all her weight.

She broke free from his pin, from his one arm that had pinned her down. Only her upper body was free. His knees, hard and knobby, were still pressing into her thighs.

Rose's hands went for his gun.

But it was too late.

The stranger pulled the trigger. The revolver discharged.

The bullet struck Rose in the arm.

The pain surprised her, sending a shock of adrenaline through her whole system.

She'd been shot, something that she never would have thought remotely possible in her previous life. Getting shot was something that happened only to people in the newspapers, only to criminals and cops and soldiers. Not to people like Rose.

Rose didn't let her surprise stop her. She had both hands around the stranger's gun.

He didn't want to let go.

Rose pried at his fingers.

She bent her neck, craning it, getting her mouth right against the stranger's exposed wrist.

She bit him. Hard, sinking her teeth into his flesh.

The stranger screamed. His grip on his gun loosened.

Rose seized the opportunity. She managed to get the gun away from his grasp.

The stranger didn't let his pain stand much in his way. His hands came towards her. Fast.

He didn't go for the gun. Instead, he went for her throat.

Rose felt his large, strong hands tighten around her throat.

She couldn't see what she was doing. The gun was in her hands, but it was wedged between their two bodies. He was pressing down against her again with all his weight, his hands never leaving her neck.

Rose knew she didn't have much time. A few more seconds and she'd lose consciousness.

The fingers around her neck tightened.

Squished between their bodies, the gun was pointed to the side.

It took all of Rose's strength to get the gun pointed slightly to the sky. That way when she pulled the trigger, the bullet would hit the stranger.

It didn't seem like she could do it. His body was too heavy. Her hands felt weak. The arm that had been shot didn't seem to be working quite right. It was incredibly weak.

Finally, with one last desperate effort, she got it.

The gun was angled slightly up. She hoped. She still couldn't see it at all.

Rose squeezed the trigger.

The recoil was intense, sending pain down her already-injured arm.

The noise of the gun was defending.

The hands around her throat loosened up immediately.

The stranger's face was right up against hers. She'd never forget the expression it wore.

He was dead. Or just about dead.

Rose could barely get the body off of her own. It took all her effort, as well as ignoring the pain in her arm. But she got him off. He rolled over into the snow onto his back, no life left in his face.

Rose scrambled to her feet. She was covered in snow and blood. Her throat was intensely sore. The gun was still in her hand.

"Jake!"

She scrambled over through the snow to Jake, who was lying completely still.

"Jake! Say something!"

Rose dropped down onto her knees, setting the gun down into the snow. With the hand of her good arm, she pawed frantically at Jake's face.

But there was no life in it.

Jake wouldn't answer her anymore.

Rose wasn't going to give up.

Despite her bad arm, she began pumping up and down on Jake's heart with both hands. She didn't know how to properly execute the maneuver she was trying to do. After all, she'd never studied first aid.

It was futile.

Jake was dead.

Rose kissed Jake's lifeless lips, which had already grown cold, and then sank down into the snow. She curled herself up into a little ball, pressing herself against Jake's dead body.

The man she was supposed to spend the rest of her life with was dead.

Rose's face was pressed into the freezing snow. She began sinking down into a tumultuous depression. The pain in her arm was nothing compared to the anger and despair raging inside her mind.

She stayed like that for a good ten minutes, sinking deeper and deeper into complete hopelessness.

But her thoughts started to shift.

Rose didn't know what it was. Or where it'd come from.

She knew it wasn't quite hope.

But it was something.

She had to go on. She had to continue.

She had to try to stay alive.

She was going to act.

Maybe it'd been listening to Max over the last week. Maybe his attitude had rubbed off on her in some subtle way. Maybe it'd been spending time with the new group of people, the group who always managed to go, go, go, the group that never stopped when the situation seemed completely impossible, completely hopeless.

She rose slowly to her feet.

The pain in her arm was intense. She unzipped her jacket to examine the wound. She didn't know what to make of it. This was her first encounter with bullet wounds.

It was more strange than horrifying to see her own flesh injured in such a way. Rarely in her life had she ever had a serious injury. She'd never even accidentally cut herself on a knife.

The bleeding didn't seem to be too bad. At least not yet.

Since Rose didn't know how to stop the bleeding, she decided to ignore the wound for now and try to get back to camp.

The revolver lay partially-buried in the snow. Rose reached down with her good arm and grabbed it.

Rose took one last glance at Jake. There was nothing she could do for him now. Or his body. She'd come back with the others to give him a proper burial.

She felt a pang of guilt in her chest as she turned away from Jake's body. She was leaving him out here like he was a dead animal.

But Jake would have wanted it this way. He would have wanted her to continue.

Rose passed the man she'd shot. He had another gun on his back. Some kind of huge rifle. Rose didn't think she'd be able to carry it with her injury, and she didn't know how to use it, so she left it.

She didn't think to look in the man's pockets, or his small sack, for anything useful. The only thing on her mind now was to get back to camp.

Rose set off, her boots wading through the snow that had started to ice over in the cold.

It was a long way back to camp. But Rose was confident she could find her way back. The moon was bright, and she had no trouble seeing.

Rose kept the gun ready, her finger on the trigger in case she encountered someone else. She knew she had to keep her guard up.

It wasn't until she'd been walking for a good five minutes, all the while not turning around once, that Rose realized how exhausted she was. The adrenaline in her system had started to die down slightly, allowing her to feel her exhaustion. She'd been through more than she'd ever been through before.

Suddenly, she heard something to her right.

Rose turned just in time to see something darting out from behind a tree.

Rose stood her ground. She wasn't going to back down. She'd fight if she had to.

She couldn't yet quite see what it was. The trees were in the way. It was just sound now.

Rose stood with her legs wide and raised the gun with her one good arm. She tried to hold it as steady as she could.

But it wasn't a person. It wasn't an enemy.

It was a dog. Nothing more than a dog. Big and furry, with pointed ears. Probably a German Shepard. The dog had seen better days. It was skinny, to the point of looking underfed. Its fur was matted in places, not to mention filthy. But despite the dog's bedraggled appearance, there wasn't a trace of malice in its features or movements.

Rose slowly lowered her gun, and stared in wonder at the dog, who looked back at her, cautiously approaching.

19

MAX

There wasn't much time.

Max was taking up the rear, running behind Mandy and James. All three ran in all-out sprints. Max's leg was killing him, but he was doing everything he could to not let it slow him down.

Max had chosen the positions carefully. If everything worked out, they'd be slightly behind and off to the side of the enemy.

If there was one thing Max had learned, it was that things rarely went the way they were supposed to. He'd have to be on his toes, on the top of his game. But expecting the unexpected was easier said than done.

Up ahead, Max saw Mandy dart behind a tree. She moved swiftly, getting onto one knee, getting her rifle into position.

There was some noise off in the direction the enemy was expected to come. Max couldn't see them yet. But there wasn't much time.

James was next. He ducked behind his tree.

Max took the last tree, the one closest to the camp, and

closest to where the enemy would probably be. He was about twenty feet from James. It was another twenty feet or so to Mandy.

Max glanced at James, who glanced back, and gave a stiff nod. There was nothing but grim determination on James's face.

Max hoped that'd be enough.

Not that there was time to hope. Only time to act.

Max wasn't sure how much ammo he had left in his Glock. Some of it was spent. He knew that much. He was about to throw a spare magazine into the Glock, but that was right when he saw them.

They were walking through the snow slowly, keeping low to the ground. They wore large white parkas. Max remembered that he'd seen those very same parkas in the compound in one of the gear rooms.

The men carried semi-automatics, and by the way they held them, it seemed like they knew what they were doing with them.

James and Mandy were glancing over at Max, waiting for the signal. They should have been keeping their eyes more on the men.

The plan had sounded good. It had sounded like it would work.

But now that Max was in it, he realized once again that while he may have been practically minded, he was really nothing more than an office worker. Sure, he was turning into something much more. The situations were forcing him to adapt. But he hadn't been in the military. He didn't have years of experience in tactical situations.

He felt like a fool, and his heart sank. There was no reason that the men would continue firing at the campsite once Max and the others opened fire on them. No, the enemy would direct their fire to the trees where Max hid.

But...

All they really needed was that early advantage, that element of surprise, those precious seconds in which they could get off the initial shots.

Max didn't let hopelessness get to him. He didn't let himself worry that his plan might have put all his friends in danger. He didn't let himself dwell on the fact that he might have killed them all. Or that they might have been better off running into the woods, like someone had suggested.

There was only one way to make this work.

And that was to act.

The gunfire popped through the night. The enemy was in position, all of them crouching, firing at the van and the tent.

Max gave the signal, throwing his right hand down.

Mandy and James saw it.

The idea was to open fire at the same time. But real synchronization was hard.

Max's rifle pressed against him, providing an almost comforting feeling.

James or Mandy's gun rang out.

One of the enemy fell, his body tumbling down into the snow. The shot had been good.

Max had one of them in his crosshairs. He took a deep breath and squeezed the trigger.

The man fell. A good hit.

The enemies were shouting, trying to make sense of the situation. They were scattering, trying to fall back into the shelter of the trees.

Max couldn't tell how many of them there were. There? Four?

Another shot rang out, probably from James.

It missed.

The enemies had retreated into the shadows of the trees, where the moonlight wasn't as bright. Max couldn't see them well, except for vague shadows that danced across the snow.

It was a good position for the enemy. They were close enough to keep up an attack, but well hidden enough to make it difficult to hit with a single shot. After all, Max and the others had no night vision, no flashlights, nothing to help them see through the twisting shadows.

Max quickly ducked his head back behind his tree.

Bullets slammed into the thick tree trunk behind which Max hid. Chips of wood and icy snow flew into the air. The noise was defending.

Max stayed as still as he could until the gunfire abated.

Max's position was known. But he hadn't been hit. He glanced over at James and Mandy. They hadn't been hit either.

Max had been right to worry. The plan had worked, but only partially. Now they were behind the trees, pinned by gunfire. The enemy knew they weren't at the camp. They knew where they were, and how to get them.

Max had to act. He couldn't let his own plan kill his friends.

Another burst of gunfire hit the tree trunk.

Max stayed completely behind the tree, glancing again over at James and Mandy. They were looking at him, obviously wondering what to do. Simply popping out from behind the tree with their rifles would almost certainly mean death.

Max wished he knew how many there were.

What he did know was there were enough to keep Max, Mandy and James pinned there behind the trees, while also sending someone over to finish hem off. And for all Max knew, the enemy could simply slowly approach, closing the gap, while keeping up the gunfire.

Hunting rifles were no match for the enemies' firepower.

Max's pulse was racing.

He knew what he had to do.

He knew where the enemy was.

It was now or never.

Right after the next burst of gunfire, he'd make his move.

Max held up his hand, signaling to James and Mandy to stay put.

The seconds seemed to drag on. The night was, for those brief moments, silent.

Max's heart was pounding.

He heard the gunfire. Plenty of it was poorly aimed, slamming into the snow. Chips of icy snow rained against Max's pant leg. Only mildly uncomfortable.

The burst ended.

Max didn't wait.

He sprang forward, pushing himself off the tree and the ground. He ran forward, sprinting as fast as he could. He ignored the stabbing pain in his leg that was only getting worse the more the night wore on.

He heard the gunfire. It only pushed him harder. He didn't look back.

There was a tree five feet in front of him.

He was almost there. The world around him seemed

to have shrunk down, leaving nothing but tunnel vision created by the adrenaline that flooded him.

Max's feet were slamming through the thin icy layer on top of the snow, hitting the ground heavily.

Something happened. His boot hit something. A root? He didn't know, and there wasn't time to wonder.

Max tripped, his body falling forward.

Instinctively, Max reached out with both hands to brace his fall. His rifle, which he had been holding in one hand as he ran, fell into the snow.

Max hit the ground hard. One of his hands slipped, and his forehead made harsh contact with something. A rock or a root.

In the movies, the heroes often lay still, hoping they wouldn't be seen in the darkness.

Max didn't have that luxury. He knew he had to move. This wasn't the movies. And movies didn't even exist anymore in any practical sense.

Max was up in a flash, just as he heard the gunfire.

He didn't know if he'd make it.

But he was going to try.

Time moved in slow motion. Max had never run harder in his life.

He reached the tree just in time, throwing himself behind it. Bullets rained down around him, and he pulled his arms and legs close to his torso, for fear they'd be struck.

He stayed perfectly still.

But his mind turned away from himself and his predicament. It turned towards Mandy and James.

If Max didn't take out the enemy in time, Mandy and James wouldn't last. Not where they were.

And there was something else to worry about as well.

James, taking his cue from Max, seemed to want to always be the hero. He wanted to risk himself to save the day. He was impulsive, and too young to fully understand the consequences of his actions.

If James decided to make a run for it, the whole plan would be lost.

Max didn't want to shout a command at James. It would only give the enemy more information than Max wanted them to have.

Max would have to hope that James would stay put. And keep fighting. When the opportunity came up, that was. There wasn't much James or Mandy could do now except stay under cover.

They'd have to wait for Max to sneak up around the enemy from the side and take them out. That would give them a chance to act.

Hopefully.

Once again, it seemed like everything fell on Max's shoulders.

It was all up to him.

Max gritted his teeth as he looked beyond, towards the next tree on his path. Just one more tree to go, and he'd be out of range.

Max's rifle lay mere feet away, but Max didn't dare go for it. He'd have to make due with just his Glock.

That was fine. It'd gotten him through plenty of tense situations. Dangerous ones.

But worse than this?

Max didn't know. And he didn't care. He didn't see the point at looking at things like that. The only thing to do was get to that next tree.

20

GEORGIA

Georgia hated being dragged along like that. It was a blow to her psychology to not be able to run under her own steam. What really bothered her was that it put the others in danger. More danger than they needed right now. Things were bad enough.

And they were about to get worse.

"Let's hope Max knows what he's doing," said Cynthia.

Georgia hadn't yet gotten used to Cynthia's temperament. It was a strange one, that was for sure, always making comments at the worst possible times.

They'd thrown themselves down behind the trees. Turning her head, Georgia could see figures approaching. The figures kept in the shadows, their silhouettes only appearing occasionally.

Georgia gave Cynthia the sign to shut up. Hopefully she'd listen.

Georgia may not have been able to walk. She may not have been able to run. But she could shoot. She'd regained most of her strength. It was only a matter of time before she'd was running again.

For now, she could shoot. That was all she needed to do.

She may have just had a hunting rifle. But she knew how to use it.

Georgia understood why Max had split up the groups like this. It was the most practical thing to do. But still, Georgia was stuck with people who were definitely not experts. In some sense, they barely knew what they were doing. In comparison, at least, to someone who had spent their whole life with guns.

Any minute now, it'd be time. They'd have to take out a lot of them right away. They couldn't let themselves get stuck in a firefight. Otherwise there'd be no way out.

Georgia counted the shadows, trying to make sense of how many men there were.

Georgia glanced back at Sadie. She was worried about her. Her daughter couldn't get shot. She just couldn't. In a way, it was better that James was with Max. Georgia still worried about him, but it was a little less direct this way.

If both her kids were here, Georgia would have been able to fight less effectively. She would have been too worried. She'd denied it to herself for a long time, telling herself that her kids only made her fight harder, that it only made her tougher. But it wasn't the truth. She realized that now, as she looked as Sadie's small form there in the semi-darkness. Sadie was just a child. She didn't deserve this.

"Sadie," hissed Georgia. "Get back farther."

"This is a good position, Mom," hissed Sadie back, staying where she was.

"Shh," hissed Cynthia. "You two want to get us all killed?"

John remained silent, his gaze aimed at the men slinking through the shadows.

"They're almost into position," whispered Georgia.

"Shouldn't we open fire now?" hissed Cynthia.

"No. We wait until they get into position."

"But why, wouldn't it be better..."

"Just do it," said Georgia. She had little patience now for questions. She was in charge, and they were going to follow her plan, whether or not they liked it.

Georgia was watching the men carefully. There were three of them.

Three...

Something seemed strange about that.

Georgia could have sworn she'd counted four shadows earlier.

Maybe it was a trick of the light. Maybe it was a trick of memory.

Or maybe one had snuck off somewhere.

The three men were close to the camp, kneeling down, getting ready. They were waiting for something, something that didn't seem to be coming.

Suddenly, gunfire rang out in the distance. It was Max, hopefully doing well. Thoughts of James flashed through Georgia's mind. Better to ignore it.

"OK!" hissed Georgia. "Now!"

Georgia already had her target in her sights. She squeezed the trigger. The rifle kicked. The recoil always felt good to her, comforting rather than harsh.

A perfect shot to the head.

The rifles rang out around her.

The other two men fell. They hadn't even had the chance to return fire.

"Keep an eye on our surroundings," hissed Georgia.

She had the fallen men in her scope. One was dead. One wasn't.

Georgia didn't know if it was an act of kindness, putting him out of his misery, or whether it was a purely practical measure.

She didn't bother figuring it out. She pulled the trigger.

"We got them all!" whispered Cynthia, sounding excited. But thankfully not excited and triumphant enough to speak at full volume.

Georgia was more cautious in her approach. "Keep your eyes peeled," said Georgia. "There could be more..."

"Why? There were three, right?"

"I think so..." said Georgia. Maybe that fourth shadow had just been her imagination. A trick of her mind and nothing more.

"I think I saw a fourth," whispered John, finally speaking, his deep male voice seeming to rumble across the cold air.

Shit. If John had seen one, too...

"I think you're right, John," said Georgia. "I think I saw another one too. A fourth."

"This is just what we need," muttered Cynthia.

"Mom," said Sadie. "What do we do?" Her voice sounded scared, becoming something of a high-pitched whimper.

The distant gunfire continued, bursts of it roaring across the cold night. Max's fight hadn't gone as easily as theirs had.

Although maybe theirs wasn't over yet.

"Max needs help. I can't make it quickly enough..."

"I'll go," said John, interrupting her. He was already standing up.

Georgia didn't know what to do. Should she send just John alone? She couldn't send Sadie into a situation like that. But if she sent Cynthia with him, it would just be herself and Sadie left behind, left to face the shadow that had disappeared, slinking away into the night to save his own skin, possibly more dangerous than all the others.

Normally, it wouldn't have been a problem. But Georgia had to remember she was injured. She wasn't completely herself. Not physically. And maybe not mentally either. She knew she'd become more cautious, maybe more timid. The injury had gotten to her. Everything had gotten to her. There simply wasn't a way to be through what they'd been through and not come out affected.

And it wasn't like it ever ended.

It was one life or death situation after another. There was no way it couldn't affect a person. The trick was to not let it crush you, let it pummel you relentlessly into the dirt and mud.

Georgia needed Cynthia there.

She looked at John. "Go," she said.

"I'm going too," said Cynthia, standing up.

"You're staying here," said Georgia.

"But..."

"We need you," said Georgia.

She could have given her a strict order. She could have dared her to disobey. But the truth worked better.

John looked at Cynthia, and then darted off through the trees, heading towards his brother.

21

MARSHAL

Marshal was no fool.

He hadn't gotten as far as he had in life by not understanding risk and reward.

He'd learned early on to only get into fights that he knew he could win. It'd served him well in life, particularly in prison.

He'd seen countless guys get carried out dead from the prison. They were guys who didn't understand what Marshal understood. They were guys who, often enough, had known they hadn't stood a chance. But they'd gone in anyway. They'd gone for the fight, heading right for the opponent's throat, even when it didn't do them any good. They were guys who'd been out to prove themselves, to make a name for themselves.

No one reminded Marshal more of those guys than Anton.

Anton was too easy to read. He was desperate for power, desperate to prop his image up.

But he didn't know shit.

And that wasn't even the start of his problems.

The whole trip, Marshal had let Anton take the reins. He'd let Anton think that he would simply go along with everything. He'd told Anton that Anton was the boss, and that he wouldn't dare interfere with his own plans.

And that was true.

To a certain extent.

The other guys from the compound didn't seem sure about Anton. But they certainly weren't ready to follow Marshal instead. They weren't ready for a mutiny, so Marshal didn't try. That was a fight he knew he wouldn't have won. And what would have been the point, anyway?

Marshal had told his men he'd take up the rear. He'd told them to get into position, and as they were walking, he'd simply slipped off. They hadn't noticed him. Not until it was too late.

Marshal had hidden between the trees, deep in the shadows, and watched the three men under his command get shot. Marshal hadn't lifted a finger to defend them. He'd saved himself. That's what was important.

But that wasn't all he was after.

Seeing the three men die like that had given Marshal a certain satisfaction. He felt it in his chest, a feeling of happiness that seemed to swell through him. A smile, a true smile, formed slowly on his face.

Marshal didn't have those feelings often. In fact, he hadn't felt anything at all until he'd discovered his ability to inflict pain. It'd been when he'd been young, playing with the family dog. Out of what had started as sheer curiosity, Marshal had stomped on the dog's paw with his sneaker. The dog had squealed in pain, and given Marshal a look that he'd never forget.

He never forgot that feeling either, that happiness that, before his discovery, had been so foreign to him.

Early on, he'd learned to fake smiles, fake happiness. Even laughter and sadness. He knew exactly how to mimic the facial expressions and emotions of others. But inside, he felt nothing. Nothing at all. He'd known, even as a child, that they would have sent him somewhere, that his life would ever be the same if he admitted to anyone that he was at all different.

Marshal had faked his way through school. He'd fooled his parents and the teachers. He'd fooled most of his peers. But the people he couldn't fool were his friends. Once people got close enough to him, they tended to realize that something was wrong, that something was off. They sensed somehow that Marshal was different. He didn't give the same responses other kids did. No matter how good he was at faking emotions, there were some responses and things that he just couldn't fake.

So the other students had respected him, but also tended to keep their distance. He wasn't a loner, but had leaned in that direction.

At some point along the way through his schooling, Marshal had decided he'd get to the bottom of himself. He'd wanted to figure out what made his own mind tick. He wanted to understand why he was different. Eventually, this interest had let to psychology textbooks, found on a dusty shelf of some teacher's shelf, probably left over from her college days.

Late at night with the textbooks, Marshal had made the discovery. The term "psychopath," had, at first, seemed like it fit him the best. But then he found "sociopath." The difference, according to the textbook, was slight. Psychopaths, though, tended to have lower intelligence scores than sociopaths. Sociopaths appeared, on the outside, completely normal. But inside, they were different. Their brains and minds were different, and they fit superficially into society very well.

Marshal knew he wasn't dumb. In fact, he'd been given an IQ test in school, and scored in the 99th percentile. The teachers had arranged a meeting with his parents, and told them he belonged in the gifted program. His parents, not believing that their son Marshal was exceptional in any way, refused. They said they wanted him to have a normal experience, just like any other kid.

Marshal had resented them for that. He'd written about it in his journal, the one he'd kept since he was a kid. He put everything in that journal, every thought he could remember. He wrote about his struggles trying to fake emotions, about the way he felt nothing, and about the way hurting animals made him feel something, that fleeing happiness that was, otherwise, impossible to capture.

His parents had found the journal on his seventeenth birthday. They'd been beyond furious. His mother had cried, and his father had called him a freak of nature, telling him that he didn't want to see him ever again. They'd kicked him out of the house with nothing more than the clothes on his back.

That was when Marshal's path had strongly diverged from his peers. He'd stopped going to school. He'd spent weeks on the street, wandering through South Philadelphia, sleeping under bridges and above heating grates.

Life on the street had provided plenty of opportunities for him to pursue his enthusiasm for inflicting pain. On the street, there'd been no parents, no teachers. No one was monitoring what happened. Police presence had been minimal on the back streets where Marshal spent his time. The world of the homeless had been, for the most part, un-policed.

Marshal had started slow, torturing stray animals he'd found. He remembered his first experience vividly, luring a stray cat to his side with soft words and the promise of a can of tunafish Marshal had stolen from a corner store. Then Marshal's strong hands had tightened themselves around the cat's neck. The feeling never left him, and he went on, looking for the next high. He'd moved on to people. Not killing them. But hurting them.

Killing animals and injuring people had been enough nourishment for his twisted mind. For a while.

Eventually, he'd become the go-to man for various gangs. When they'd wanted to bring about particularly harsh "justice," they'd bring out Marshal, knowing that no one knew the dance of death and pain like he did.

That's what had landed Marshal in jail.

The EMP had been, he'd thought, a new beginning. Not just a get-out-of-jail free card. But something more. Much more. Marshal had seen the EMP as a return to man's natural chaotic state. It was life on the streets all over again. Only more so. More intense.

No police, no military. No government. No nothing. It all meant, to Marshal, that he could pursue his passion for pain in ways he'd never previously imagined. He'd roamed the streets, wild, inflicting pain whenever he wanted to. He'd killed often, and he'd been happy.

But he'd also been smart about it. He'd never risked his own safety in pursuit of his passion. In that way, he was reserved.

He'd also recognize, soon enough, that the world wouldn't remain ungoverned. To his dismay, the militia started to take over almost immediately. In the weeks following the EMP, the militia had grown more powerful, stricter, and more regimented.

The only thing to do was to join. Marshal had worked his way up. His intelligence was his primary asset, not to mention the reputation he'd gained in prison as someone you didn't want to mess with if you wanted to stay alive.

Marshal was a realist. He knew he couldn't exist the way he wanted to outside the militia. He also knew that the militia was too strictly controlled to let him run wild the way he wanted to.

So he'd resolved to play the game again. To the militia, he'd present himself as a rule-following man dedicated to the growth and power of the militia. Meanwhile, privately, he'd do everything he could to cause chaos and pain. He'd use his rising reputation within the militia to seek out opportunities in which he could pursue his passion.

And he'd keep no journal. There'd be no way to discover his true intentions, the interior of his dark mind. He'd learned that lesson the hard way. He'd learned it for good.

Marshal had enjoyed seeing his companions get gunned down on the dirt bikes. It'd been something, but not quite enough. Marshal had been finding that the more pain he could inflict or witness, the more he craved it. It was like a drug, and he felt like he'd merely just whet his appetite.

There was gunfire in the distance. Presumably Anton was fighting for his life. Or the other way around.

Marshal didn't particularly care which way the fight turned out. He didn't care which side won, so long as he could move in afterwards like a specter and kill those who remained.

Whatever happened, Marshal would be there at the

end. He'd hide in the shadows until the gunfire ceased. Then, when the survivors, whoever they were, thought everything was fine, and that they were safe, Marshal would move in and enjoy himself.

Marshal had never cared about the radios. Or about forming an alliance with the compound. It had all just been a ruse. He'd have his fun here, and then slowly make his way back to the suburbs of Philadelphia, where he'd deliver a completely false but completely believable report about the state of things in the western part of the state. Despite what he'd told Anton, he knew damn well how to get back. His ignorance had, like everything else, just been an act.

Marshal scanned the trees from his hiding place. Clouds were drifting in front of the moon, blocking its light.

Soon it would be time.

For now, he'd wait.

22

MAX

Max had gotten beyond the bursts of gunfire. He didn't know how he'd survived, but he didn't stop to ponder his good luck. Not even for a moment.

He'd gotten to safety. The night was darker now. Clouds covered the moon. Max was lost in the dark shadows where the trees were dense. All he had to do now was sneak around from the side, attack the enemies from a direction they weren't expecting.

But he had to move fast.

The gunfire continued. Max heard the clear sound of a hunting rifle discharging. Hopefully James had stayed in place, but it sounded like he was firing back when he could. Max knew that meant that James was taking a huge risk, sticking himself into visibility in order to fire back.

He had guts, that kid. Max hoped it didn't get him killed.

It would help Max. It would serve as a distraction.

Max just didn't know how long James could keep it up.

Two rifle sounds now. Definitely hunting rifles. Mandy had joined in.

Max was already on the move, and he picked up his pace. His boots crunched through the snow.

Blood trickled down from his forehead all the way to his mouth. He tasted it, and spit it into the snow. He'd knocked his forehead pretty hard. But it wasn't enough to deter him. Not a lot was.

The fall had hurt his ribs. He doubted he'd broken one.

Max clutched his Glock in his right hand. As he moved, his cold hand fumbled inside his jacket for a spare magazine.

He was expecting to feel the magazine against his hand. But instead, there was nothing.

At first, he thought his hand had just gone numb with cold. Or from injury, when he'd fallen on it. After all, there were some small cuts on hands that he'd ignored. It was possible that he'd sliced through some nerves and not realize it.

But, no, Max switched hands, handing the Glock over to himself, and there was still nothing. He opened up his jacket, unzipping it completely.

Max found the problem. There was no longer a bottom to the jacket's internal pocket. Instead there was just frayed fabric. Maybe it had torn during his fall. Or maybe it'd happened earlier. Whenever it had happened, the spare magazines had fallen right out of his jacket.

Max looked back in the direction he'd come.

No sign of the spare magazines.

If Max couldn't see them from where he was, the magazines were either where he'd fallen, right in range of the enemy, or somewhere else entirely. It would take too long to find them. And be too dangerous.

Max had to continue.

Max remove the magazine from his Glock and checked it. Four rounds left.

Well, thought Max, that'd have to be enough.

Ignoring the pain in his legs, his forehead, and his ribs, Max ran forward as fast he could into the night.

He didn't bother trying to be quiet. Not yet. Max ran through the woods in a large semi-circle. He calculated the path roughly in his head, visualizing the scene from a bird's eye view. He had to manage risk and time. He had to get there fast. But if they spotted him in the process, the whole plan would be ruined.

If he was spotted, he'd be shot. But it wasn't his life he was worried about. It was Mandy and James's. Not to mention Georgia, his brother, and the others. Max didn't know what was happening over there on the other side. But he knew that if he didn't do what he had to do, the likelihood of the others surviving was slimmer.

Max pushed back his jacket sleeve to see his watch. The luminescent hands were just barely visible in the clouded moonlight. Russian watches had never been known for their lume.

It'd been ten minutes so far. Max was almost there. He could see the figures up ahead. He heard the gunfire still. But he hadn't heard the hunting rifle. At least, he didn't think so. It was hard to distinguish, after all, individual firearms through the cacophony of sound that ripped sporadically through the night.

He hoped Mandy and James were still alive. He hoped they weren't lying behind their trees, bleeding out into the snow.

But whether or not they were didn't change what he was going to do next.

Max was approaching from behind. He slowed his pace. He eased his boots onto the snow, trying to eliminate the crunching noise they made.

Max's finger was on the trigger.

Three figures were in front of him. They were completely focused on Mandy and James. They didn't turn around once. They didn't even glance from side to side.

They were sloppy. That was their business. It was Max's job to take advantage of whatever opportunity they left him.

Max took a deep breath. There was so much at stake. He couldn't let his emotions run away from him. He needed to keep a calm, cool head and do what he needed to do. He needed to act swiftly.

By approaching the enemy from behind, Max knew he'd be putting himself directly in the path of Mandy and James's rifles. It was a risk that he needed to take. Hopefully Mandy and James, despite the desperate situation, wouldn't shoot too hastily. Hopefully they wouldn't shoot Max.

But if they did, then Max was willing to live with that.

He knew he was up against impossible odds. If he came out of this alive, he'd be surprised.

Three men, even if they were facing the wrong direction, were too much for him to tackle on his own. Especially when all he had was his Glock with four bullets, a knife, and his own cunning. He had a busted leg, and his ribs and head hurt. The enemy was heavily armed. All they had to do was spin around and pump Max full of bullets.

But Max had to try.

His body was rebelling against the thought of death. No matter how determined someone was, or how brave, there was a desperate drive inside them, telling them that they had to live, that they had to do whatever it took to stay alive.

There were few things in the world that could override that instinct.

And one of them was saving others.

Max wasn't doing this for himself. He was doing it was Mandy, Georgia, her kids, his brother, and Cynthia. He was doing it for them.

He didn't have a fatalistic attitude. That simply wouldn't have helped him. If he was completely convinced that he was doing to die, then he probably would.

Instead, the thing to do, he knew, was to trick himself. He had to convince himself it would come off fine. The plan would go off without a hitch.

If James and Mandy had a break from the constant gunfire that was keeping them pinned in place, they might just be able to get off some clean shots of their own.

The only way to know was to find out. There wasn't any way to communicate with them. The radios back at camp weren't portable. They weren't made for this kind of situation.

Max slunk forward, walking as slowly and silently as he could. One noise and he'd be out of time. He needed to shoot first. That was the only way this could work.

The gunfire still punctuated the night. Mandy and James weren't firing. Max hoped, once again, that they were still alive. Even if they weren't, Max still had to do this. He still had to think of Georgia, John, and the others.

A thick tree was close by, off to Max's right. He was ready to dive behind it. But there might not be time.

It was now or never. Max was close. One of the enemy was fishing for a spare clip.

Max took careful aim, right at the back one of their heads.

Max squeezed the trigger. The Glock recoiled. It was a good feeling. Harsh, but comforting.

The man fell. The shot had been perfect, his body crumpling into the snow. But that was the last of Max's worries.

The two others spun around. Everything seemed, once again, to be happening in slow motion. Max had to make a split second decision. Did he train his Glock on the second man? Or did he dash behind the tree?

He opted for the second.

He threw himself behind the tree.

Just in time.

Gunfire erupted. Loud bursts. Bullets cut into the bark behind him, and the snow by his feet.

Come on, thought Max. This is your time, James and Mandy.

Max had done this for them.

But there was no crack of the hunting rifles.

Max feared the worst.

A surge of energy suddenly filled him. Emotions flooded his body. Thoughts of revenge swelled through him.

His normal calm-under-pressure pattern had failed him.

These men had killed James and Mandy.

Max threw himself out from behind the tree.

He saw the two men facing him. He squeezed the trigger of his Glock. Three times. In rapid succession.

The first man fell. The bullets had struck him in the throat and the chest.

The other man still stood. Max had missed.

Max squeezed the trigger again.

Btu he was out of ammo.

Long ago, before the EMP, Max had read the Tueller Drill studies, first published in SWAT magazine in 1983. They described what happened when a man with a knife charged a man with a gun. Surprisingly, the man with the knife had a chance. If he could run fast enough, he could attack before the gun-wielding man could get off a shot.

Not a very good chance, though.

With Max's leg the way it was, the odds were distinctly not in his favor.

To make it worse, there wasn't time to get his knife out from his pocket and unfold it. No matter how fast he was at deploying it, it didn't matter.

All this information had been engrained in Max's mind for a long, long time.

He knew it wouldn't work.

But he was so filled with rage he didn't care.

Max charged forward. He still held the Glock in his hand. It was heavy enough to use as a weapon. It wasn't a knife, but it was something.

The man in front of him already had his gun raised. An expression of surprise came over his face.

Max wasn't going to make it.

He was sprinting right towards his certain death.

Before the enemy could get off a shot, a crack rang out.

A hunting rifle.

The man fell.

There was hope now. Mandy or James was alive. Or maybe both of them were. Was that too much to hope for?

Max bent down, taking the gun from the man. He wasn't dead. His grip was still strong enough to try to resist.

Max yanked on the gun and got it free. He didn't waste any time. The weight of the gun felt good in his hands. At point blank range, Max pulled the trigger, sending a single round through the man's heart.

Max couldn't believe it. He was alive. The enemies were dead.

Max had let rage and thoughts of revenge overtake him, and yet he hadn't died, even though he should.

Max wasn't going to make the same mistake again. He desperately wanted to check on Mandy and James. If they needed help, he needed to be there for them.

But Max knew that he couldn't count on the battle being over.

He couldn't be careless. He wasn't going to let his emotions take over again.

For the first time since this had all started, Max felt the cold. It was even colder now than when it had been snowing. The temperature must have been approaching the single digits. A gust of wind blew in, causing Max to shiver.

The dead men in front of him would provide a wealth of equipment. Not just guns, but parkas, hats, socks, and boots. Sure, the parkas might be stained with blood. That was fine with Max, though.

He'd have to wait.

The night was silent once again. Silent and cold.

Crouched there on the ground, the dead man's gun in his hands, Max looked through the darkness.

The clouds had come along in full force, covering the moon. It was darker than before.

Max was determined to be cautious. After all, there could be more men out there.

But Max saw no one.

Nothing moved. There was no sound.

Everything was quiet.

Max heard his own boots crunching on the snow as he stood up. He'd come back to the bodies later.

He started moving across the silent, dark woods, heading towards Max and Mandy. He kept his eyes scanning the surroundings as he walked.

He was ready.

But it wasn't enough.

Movement behind him. He heard it too late. Someone was rushing out from behind a tree.

Something hard hit Max in the head. His field of vision swam, and pain seared through his skull.

Btu he didn't lose consciousness.

Holding the gun with both hands, Max jammed it backwards, hoping to hit his attacker with the butt of the gun.

Max missed.

Something hard hit Max in the back. He reeled in pain, about to fall forward, but he caught himself, putting his left leg out first.

Max barely held onto his balance. But he managed to spin around.

His attacker was a man about his age with a severe face. He wore the same clothing as the others. He lunged forward at Max, swinging his right fist in a wide arc.

Max's head was spinning. His balance wasn't good.

Instead of trying to duck the blow, he lunged forward, throwing himself at the man's legs.

It worked. Max's shoulder slammed into the man's legs, and Max threw his arms around them, pulling back with all his strength until the man fell, flat on his back.

Max was on top of him in a flash, straddling him, pushing down with all his weight. His vision still swam. But he could see well enough to fight.

The man threw a punch. It caught Max in the cheek, pain flashing through him.

Max's face was right against his enemies. The face was familiar. It was someone from the compound.

Max was dizzy. He was losing ground. Quickly. Their hands became a messy tangle as each fought for control. The enemy was gaining. Max's vision swam. He could barely keep it all straight. It seemed to be happening too quickly.

Hands gripped Max's neck, squeezing hard, tightening.

"I wanted to get my hands on you myself," said the man. He spoke with a strange accent. Harsh sounding. The anger poured out of his voice. He could barely contain it. "I could have shot you in the back. Just like you shot my men. You've ruined everything. And now you're going to pay."

The enemy's hands occupied, Max found his own hands free. He let his right hand fall to the side. If only he hadn't lost those spare magazines. His Glock was useless now. He had a knife, but he didn't have the physical strength to use it.

The guy must have had a gun on him. All Max had to do was find it. His hands went searching, looking for a holster, patting and pawing at the enemy's parka, trying to find where it ended. He couldn't see what he was doing. All he could do was reach and search, his hand flailing blindly.

The hands gripped him even tighter. Max was moments away from losing consciousness. Moments away from death.

He had to act. Now. But he was weak. The strength was leaving his body.

"I could have shot you," growled the man. "But this is much, much better."

Max's hand hit up against something. Something smooth. Leather. He fumbled for the gun that he knew must have been there inside the holster.

The enemy didn't seem to notice. He was intent on strangling Max to death. His face was pressed up against Max's, his neck craning, his pupils small and contracted, his expression beyond intense.

Max's vision was going. But he still couldn't find the gun.

Suddenly, sounds rang out through the woods. Max barely registered them. They sounded like shouts. Max wasn't sure. He was concentrating on his hand, on finding that gun. If he could just get it, he could end this. He could put a bullet through the man's torso. He just needed that gun.

But there was nothing in the holster. His hand felt nothing but smooth leather.

A shot rang out. Loud and close. Max's ear's rang with the sound.

The hands loosened, falling away from his throat. Blood dribbled out of the enemy's mouth.

23

JOHN

John couldn't believe it. He'd made the shot. He'd had the man in his sights for long. Too long. The seconds had ticked by, seeming like an eternity. He hadn't known whether he could do it, whether he could kill the enemy and not accidentally shoot his brother.

Finally, he'd simply had to act. Max was going to die anyway.

John rushed across the snow, his boots sinking, over to Max.

"You still with us, Max?" said John, bending down and grabbing Max by the shoulders.

"Not dead yet," muttered Max.

John pulled Max to his feet. The color had drained from Max's face.

"You don't look too bad. How do you feel?"

"Fine," said Max. There was blood on his face, and pain in his eyes.

The sound of footsteps. John turned, raising his gun.

"James... Mandy..." said Max.

John didn't fire at the silhouettes running towards them. When they got into view, he could see them clearly. It was James and Mandy.

"Max!"

"He's alive!"

Max looked up at them, nodding a greeting.

"Let's get him back to camp," said John. "Here, help me."

"What happened?" said Max. "Georgia, Sadie?"

"Everyone's fine," said John. "The plan worked."

Max glanced around, looking into the woods. "There might be more out there," he said.

"Come on," said John. "Don't be ridiculous. We got them all."

Max didn't say anything.

James and Mandy still looked stunned.

"I can't believe that worked," said Mandy, speaking in hushed tones. She stared in disbelief at Max.

"I couldn't have done it without you two," said Max, nodding at them again.

Max looked unsteady on his feet, and John reached out to give him a supporting hand.

But Max shook him off.

"Just trying to help," said John.

Max didn't say anything. He was looking into the woods.

"Come on," said John. "It's only getting colder. Let's get back to camp. It's not doing you any good out here."

"Help me get this gear," said Max, gesturing to the dead man.

"We'll come back for it," said John.

But Max was already trying to take the blood-stained

parka off the corpse. He fumbled with the zipper, his hands too cold to move delicately.

"Let me get that for you, Max" said James.

Max stood up, moving aside to let James work.

Mandy stood there, shivering, opening her mouth a few times, as if she wanted to speak. But nothing came out.

Finally, the words came tumbling out of her. "I tried, Max," she said. "I wanted to shoot him... when he had his hands around your neck. But I couldn't bring myself to do it. I was too worried I'd shoot you instead. I told James not to shoot. I thought you'd get him any moment. I thought you had it..."

A single tear rolled down Mandy's cheek. She seemed pretty shaken up by the experience, by her own inability to act.

"It's fine," said Max. "You already saved me once. One of you saved me when I thought I was dead. You weren't under any obligation to do it again."

"I guess I was the least concerned about shooting Max," said John, laughing. "Sometimes it takes a brother to do something like that."

James had gotten the coat off the dead man and was going through his pockets. "His handgun's missing, but there's some good stuff here," said James, holding up a compass, a lighter, and an expensive-looking fixed blade survival knife. "He had the knife in his boot," said James.

"I don't know why he didn't just shoot me, or knife me," said Max.

John shrugged. "He was messed up. Who cares."

"Motives are important," said Max.

"Sometimes," said John. "But not when the guy's dead."

"I wish this were over," said Max. "But I don't think it is. Come on, we've got to get the rest of the gear." He gestured over in the direction of the other corpses.

"You're crazy," said John. "You're in no condition to..."

But Max was already walking away, limping, blood trickling down his face.

John, James, and Mandy exchanged a look and went scrambling to catch up with Max.

They got what they could from the corpses. The parkas were thick and warm. They'd serve well, much better than what they had. Max was still wearing the coat he'd worn all along, one that couldn't have been much protection against the frigid temperatures.

John himself could barely feel his hands. He needed to get back to the fire, back to camp. But Max insisted on retracing his steps, finding his rifle and the spare magazines that had fallen out of his jacket. Max's hands were so cold that he could barely load the magazine. But there was nothing but determination on his face, and John at that point knew better than to suggest doing it later.

It didn't take long to walk back. Max insisted on taking up the rear, refusing all help, despite his limp appearing worse than it had in a while.

"You're alive!" cried out Cynthia, rushing towards him. She threw herself against him, almost knocking him down, hugging him.

"Easy there," said John, laughing.

Georgia was there, along with her daughter, Sadie. They were both working on getting the fire restarted. Georgia was looking exhausted, which wasn't surprising, considering her injury. She was sitting there on a patch of clear earth, where the fire that had burned earlier had melted away the snow. Sadie was on her knees, following her mother's instructions, trying to get the fire back.

Bullets had ripped through the van and the tent. They hadn't provided much warmth before, and they certainly wouldn't now.

"All right," said Max, raising his voice so everyone could hear him easily. "We've won the battle. But we've got to be vigilant. We don't know what's going to happen next."

"Come on, Max," said John. "Why don't you sit down? You deserve a break."

Max ignored him, except to say, "John, you and Cynthia are on official watch. I want you there, and there." He pointed to opposite ends of the camp. "Everyone else, keep your eyes peeled. Consider yourselves on unofficial watch."

"Max," said John, approaching his brother. "Don't you think you need to rest? You almost died back there, and you're not looking good."

Max shook his head. "Any sign of Rose or Jake?" he said, speaking loudly to everyone, and ignoring John again.

Everyone shook their heads. No one had seen Rose or Jake since they'd run from the camp. No sign of them.

John was starting to get annoyed with his brother. He was acting like they were still in a critical situation, even when everything was obviously over. The enemies had been defeated. Killed. If there'd been someone else out there, they would have fought. The enemies had acted like soldiers in an army. Why would some of them hold back while their comrades got killed? It didn't make sense.

And John was getting annoyed at the way Max kept ignoring him, acting like what he was saying didn't matter.

Max was acting like he knew everything, like he knew exactly what to do.

But Max hadn't done it all by himself. Maybe he was the unofficial leader, but they'd all worked together as a team just now. And if it hadn't been for John's shot, Max would be dead right now. He thought he deserved something, some recognition.

"I'm going," said Max, suddenly.

"What?"

"I'm going to look for them," said Max.

"Come on, that's crazy. You can't leave now."

Max stared at John. There was something intense about his eyes. Something that made John feel a little uneasy.

"It's dangerous," said John.

"You said yourself there's no one out there," said Max, his voice deadpan.

"Yeah," sputtered John, looking for a rationale to back up what he was saying. "But... I mean, it is possible..."

Mandy moved over to Max, putting a comforting hand on his arm. "We're all worried about them, Max," said Mandy. "But don't you think it'd be better to wait until morning? You're too cold to fight effectively. Wait an hour or so, warm up, and when the sun rises, we'll go together."

Max nodded. "Fine," he said. "But I'm going alone."

John shot an angry look at Max. Why was he willing to take Mandy's advice, but not the advice of his own brother?

24

MARSHAL

It was colder, but the cold didn't bother Marshal the way it did other people. Sure, his body responded to it the same way as anyone else's would. He wasn't a superhero. He could get frostbite and hypothermia as easily as anyone.

But his mind was stronger than most.

Without the emotional toil, the baggage that common people carried, Marshal was free to do what he wished with his body. He could push himself harder and longer than he should have been able to. He'd learned this at an early age on the playground and in gym class at school. He'd been able to outrun anyone when it came to distance, even though he wasn't the fastest, and hadn't been the strongest.

But he was strong now. Prison life had given him the time he'd needed, as well as the resources, to sculpt his body. He'd done so unemotionally, as if he were designing a machine. He'd quickly gained a reputation as the prisoner who wouldn't quit in the gym. He'd pushed through injuries like they were nothing. When others would have taken a step back, let themselves recover, Marshal had just kept going.

It hadn't been devoid of drawbacks. Marshal's shoulder still clicked when he raised his arm, and his knee flared up on him occasionally. But he simply didn't care. He thought of his body only as a machine that he could use. He thought of his body the way he thought of everything, with no emotional attachment whatsoever.

Marshal's only drive now was to find himself pleasure. He needed a victim. He needed to inflict pain. Lots of it.

And he wasn't going to stop at just one.

No, he was going to pick them off one by one.

Marshal's "comrades," if you could call them that, were all dead. That was fine with him. They'd done their job. They'd weakened those at the camp, making them perfect prey for Marshal.

Marshal had been spying on the camp from a distance with his binoculars. Now he retreated, pushing his position farther away from the camp. He didn't want to be discovered. He needed his time. He needed to let them think they were safe.

It was almost dawn, and Marshal was hungry. But he didn't eat, even though he had food with him in his pack. Plenty of it. He did this often, not giving into hunger. He liked to have complete control over his body. Or at least feel like he did.

From behind him, Marshal heard something. It sounded like a woman's voice.

Marshal turned.

There, in the semi-darkness of pre-dawn, a young woman was wandering through the snow. A dog walked in front of her, turning back. It was as if the dog was trying to guide her, trying to show her the way.

But the woman wasn't acting normally. She didn't seem to be in her right mind.

She walked in large zigzags, ambling slowly through the snow, talking to herself.

"Almost there, Jake," she was saying, her voice now reaching Marshal clearly as she got closer. "Just a little ways to go."

Her words were muffled, as if her lips were too cold to speak properly.

She was probably suffering from hypothermia. The bitter cold had gotten to her.

Had those at the camp abandoned one of their own, left her to wander and freeze to death in the woods?

Although she didn't know it, the young woman was almost back at camp. If she continued in the direction she was aimlessly headed, guided by the dog, she'd soon be recovering from her hypothermia.

But Marshal had different plans for her.

She was perfect.

She'd be the first.

Marshal felt the excitement rising inside him. It was rare to feel this. To feel anything. These were special feelings, rare and hard to find. He craved these moments. He'd remember this.

When they'd locked him up, the prosecutors had called him a serial killer. But that wasn't how Marshal thought of himself. To him, he was just a killer. It was what he did, and what he would always do. The numbers didn't matter. Not to him, anyway.

Marshal kept his gun slung over his back as he walked towards the woman.

"Who... are... you?" she said, speaking slowly, her voice slurred.

"I'm going to help you," said Marshal, looking her right in the eye. Her eyes were a brilliant blue.

The dog, which was up ahead, turned back. It was a German Shepherd. A big one. In another time, it would have been good material for Marshal. But those times were over. He had better victims now.

"Who...." The woman started to speak again.

The dog started barking, and she stopped, letting her words trail off into the cold air.

Marshal ignored the dog's bark, continuing to stare into her eyes. She looked delirious.

The woman had stopped in her tracks, standing still, looking back and forth between the barking dog and the Marshal, swaying slightly from side to side.

"It's going to be OK," said Marshal, his voice soothing.

The dog kept barking.

"Come with me," said Marshal, offering his arm out to the woman.

But she didn't take it. She looked again at the dog.

That stupid dog. Why wouldn't it stop barking?

"Shut up!" shouted Marshal.

The dog just barked louder.

Marshal had his handgun out in a flash. He squeezed the trigger. Three times in rapid succession.

His aim was good. The dog fell to the ground, blood oozing around the wounds.

Good. That was taken care of. And he'd felt briefly good while doing it. Not enough to satisfy him. Just enough to further whet his appetite.

The woman, now behind him, seeing the dog die, let out a scream.

Marshal spun around, letting his gun arm swing with him. He hit her in the shoulder with the butt of the gun.

He'd decided against her head as a target. He didn't want to her to lose consciousness. It wouldn't give him the same feeling.

The woman screamed again. She was moving, but too slowly, reaching for a gun. Or trying to. She barely knew what she was doing. It was just pure instinct on her part.

Marshal was too fast for her. He took the gun from her hands easily. She was weak, like a child. Marshal tossed the gun aside, and punched her in the head. Not as hard as he could, but good enough to give her some pain, enough to knock some more of the fight out of her.

Marshal had been planning on dragging her away, to some safe spot, farther away from the camp.

She'd seemed so disoriented, Marshal hadn't thought she'd fight back.

But she was.

She was screaming, trying to claw at his face. One of her nails caught him, drawing a long line of blood along his cheek.

Marshal was beyond annoyed. She was supposed to go easily. Sure, some struggle sometimes made it more fun. But not this time. He was too eager for it. Too eager for the kill. He'd wanted to enjoy this one, savor it in his own way, on his own time.

The woman threw her body towards him, trying to attack him, trying to throw him off balance. There was a wild look of instinctual desperation on her face.

But she'd gotten hit too hard with hypothermia. She was off balance, and she didn't even reach Marshal. She ended up just throwing herself into the snow, falling face first and crying out in pain as the icy snow cut into her.

Marshal was on top of her in a flash. He dug his knees into her back, putting all of his weight onto her.

"You're not making this easy enough for me," said Marshal, his voice deadpan. "Nor hard enough."

She flailed at him with the one hand that wasn't stuck underneath her body. But she could barely reach him.

Marshal laughed. He was starting to feel something, that happiness that seemed to come surging back to him.

Marshal holstered his gun.

The gun was too fast. He glanced over at the dog carcass. Sure, he could injure her with a gun. He could intentionally aim for the non-vital areas.

But that wouldn't be as much fun as his knife.

He needed to get out of this what he could. She was already ruining the whole thing, mainly by being half-comatose, unable to really pose a serious challenge.

Marshal felt for the sheath at his belt, lifting up his parka to do so. He unbuttoned the single strap that kept the knife in place. It was a good one, a carbon steel survival knife issued to some European country's military. Marshal didn't know the details. He didn't care.

The knife had been liberated from some dead idiot out in the suburbs by another militia member, who hadn't shut up about the knife's advantages. He and Marshal had been on a scouting mission when they'd killed the man. Marshal had gotten so fed up listening to the story about the knife that he'd simply shot his scouting partner in the face and taken the knife for himself.

That had been back in the early days, in the early weeks after the EMP. The militia had been young. It was still young now, relatively speaking, but things had gotten more orderly. Now, there was an official roster of all members. Marshal simply couldn't go around shooting whoever he wanted, especially not other militia members. The good days were gone.

Marshal was making his own good days.

"Don't ruin this for me," muttered Marshal, as he got the knife into position. He himself wasn't quite sure what he meant.

With his free hand, Marshal grabbed the back of the woman's head. His grip was strong. He cupped the back of her skull easily. He turned her head, so she was face down in the snow and pushed. Hard. Her cries were muffled by the snow.

Marshal waited patiently, counting the seconds.

He didn't want her to pass out. Not yet.

When she was almost there, Marshal let up the pressure. She raised her face above the snow, sputtering, spitting snow from her mouth.

At that moment, right when she thought she was free from the suffering, Marshal seized her ear in one hand. He pinched the top of her ear hard, squeezing with his fingers. Pulling the ear back with one hand, he used his knife to slice slowly and carefully.

She screamed.

Blood spurted.

The ear was gone.

Marshal held the bloodied severed ear up close to his face, examining it impassively.

He was starting to feel the swell of that elusive happiness. It was working.

The woman was thrashing harder now, like some wild animal, doing everything she could to fight off Marshal, to save herself.

Marshal stayed in position, his knees still digging into her, as he considered his options.

The ideal situation would have been to take her away somewhere. Cut her up slowly and steadily, without fear of distractions. Give her as much pain as possible.

Marshal knew he was out of earshot of the camp. No matter how loudly she screamed, they wouldn't hear her.

But he was still too close to the camp to fully enjoy himself. He wouldn't be able to take his time. Someone could come along. There was that chance, no matter how unlikely, and Marshal had to be wary of it.

He'd learned his lesson once before. He'd gotten too greedy, too carless. That was back when he'd been living in the city, preying on the weak. That was how he'd gotten caught.

He wasn't going to make the same mistake again.

Marshal looked down at her thrashing body. He longed to slash it and mutilate it. Maybe even burn it. Or parts of it, at least.

But he'd have to wait.

He'd have to take what enjoyment he could from this brief encounter.

After all, there'd be others. Soon enough, too. There were plenty of men and women at the camp. Marshal would pick them off one by one. He'd take his time. They'd be easier. They'd be better victims.

"Sorry this is going to be so quick," said Marshal.

The woman screamed.

Marshal brought his knife down swiftly, stabbing her in the back, through her coat. He pulled the knife out, blood dripping off the steel. He stabbed again. And again, until she was silent, until the life had completely left her.

Marshal felt the swelling of emotion in his solar plexus. This was good, but it had only whet his taste for more. Much more.

Marshal stood up calmly and slowly. But not before

wiping the carbon steel blade carefully on the dead woman's jacket.

He looked to the sun, which had just appeared on the horizon, bringing warmth and light to the snow-covered landscape.

25

MAX

"You feeling better?" said Mandy.

Max nodded. His whole body had been stiff with cold, but a few hours by the fire, and some venison, had made him feel limber once again. Not that he wasn't exhausted. They all were.

"You weren't serious about going out alone, were you?"

Max shook his head. "No," he said.

"Why'd you say that?"

"I was serious at the time," said Max. "The cold must have gotten to me... the adrenaline from the fight. It's better to wait until there's daylight."

Max was glad he hadn't rushed out into the night looking for Jake and Rose. He still thought there could easily be more enemies out there. And, frankly, the probability that Jake and Rose had died was high.

"Good," said Mandy. "Because you know it doesn't make sense to go all cowboy and try to do everything yourself. You'll just get killed. You're the one who's always advising caution, after all. It wouldn't look very good if you got killed by not following your own advice."

Max let out a brief, muted laugh. Then he fell into silence again. Mandy too. There was, after all, nothing funny about the situation. Jake and Rose were missing. Probably dead.

"It's weird," said Mandy, speaking slowly. "It's almost like I've gotten used to this."

"To what?"

"To people going missing, turning up dead."

Max nodded. "It's tough, but..."

"Yeah, yeah," said Mandy, cutting him off. "We've got to keep going."

Max laughed again. This time, it was more of a real laugh. "I guess I say that a lot?"

Mandy's eyes twinkled. "Sometimes."

They were sitting close together, away from the fire, facing north. Most of the others were sitting by the fire.

Their guns lay beside them. The sun was rising slowly, making everything once again seem possible, giving them hope when they'd had no hope before.

Mandy leaned in, her mouth approaching Max's.

Max, for a moment, didn't move. He just stared into Mandy's eyes, which seemed to be sparkling. They were deep and beautiful. He hadn't had much time to look into her eyes in the last weeks.

This was a rare moment, one that Max promised himself he'd remember in the future, once things got rough again. They always seemed to, chaos coming rumbling in like a freight train, disrupting all their carefully calculated plans and schemes.

Max leaned in, his lips meeting hers. They kept their eyes open. For some reason, it seemed more natural that way.

"Hey!" came a gruff voice.

It was John. His boots tread heavily across the ground.

Mandy pulled quickly away from Max, quickly becoming busy removing her cap and rearranging her hair, which was had been a permanent mess for the last week. That was fine with Max. He happened to like that look.

"What is it?" said Max, turning to his brother.

John looked angry. Max could tell just by the way he moved, the way he walked. Sure, it had been a lot of years since they'd spent time together, but people didn't change that much. At least not their "tells," and the way they expressed their emotions.

"I thought you were going to strike out on your own, hunt down Jake and Rose all by yourself?"

"I thought you didn't want me to go," said Max.

"He's not going alone," said Mandy. "He just told me."

"That's right," said Max. "We need to go out in groups. I wasn't thinking clearly before."

"I'm not sure you've been thinking clearly for a while," muttered John.

"What was that?" said Max.

"You heard me."

Max stood up, facing his brother. He didn't have time for this. Whatever was bothering John probably had more to do with him than it did with Max.

"There isn't time for this," said Max. "We've got to get going."

"But there was plenty of time to sit around, waiting until dawn?"

"I don't understand what you're getting at."

"What I'm getting at is that I don't think you're such a great leader," said John, his nostrils flaring, his eyebrows narrowing. "Every decision you've made…"

"Every decision he's made has been the right one," said Mandy, interrupting him and standing up beside Max.

Max put his hand up, gesturing to Mandy that that was enough.

"I don't always make the right decisions," said Max, speaking slowly. "Sometimes there aren't any right decisions. And when I've been wrong, when I'm way off, at least I admit it. I was wrong to want to go after them myself. There, I said it."

John didn't seem to know what to say.

"Now that it's light," said Max, "we're heading out. Mandy, we'll go together. John, you take Cynthia. Everyone else will guard the camp. That is, if you're up for it."

He stared his brother right in the eyes. John didn't blink.

Finally, John nodded. Whatever his problem with Max was, he was willing to recognize a plan that made sense.

"Good," said Max. "We'll head that way, cutting a wide arc. You two can take the other direction." He pointed as he spoke. "Keep an eye out for footprints. And tell Georgia what's going on."

John nodded again. He was silent, but the anger was still on his face.

Max nodded to Mandy, and they set off, leaving John standing there.

They'd gotten ready a half hour ago, but they carried minimal gear with them. They had a rifle and handgun each and a small supply of extra food and water that they were able to fit into their parka pockets. Backpacks would only weight them down, making traversing the snow more difficult.

If things ever calmed down, Max had plans for making rudimentary snowshoes. For now, they were stuck slogging through the snow in their boots.

The temperature had risen. Not enough to melt the snow, but enough to feel significantly warmer than last night's frigid temperatures. If he'd had to guess, Max would have said it was in the high twenties. Maybe thirty.

As they walked, Mandy kept glancing at Max.

"What is it?" said Max, finally.

"Aren't you going to say anything about what happened?"

"What do you mean?"

"With your brother. With John."

Max shrugged. "What's there to say?"

"Aren't you wondering why he was so upset?"

"That's his business," said Max.

Mandy huffed. "No wonder you two didn't talk much after childhood."

Max said nothing but he picked up the pace. His leg was, strangely, feeling better. Maybe it was the weather. His head, however, hadn't stopped hurting since he'd fallen, and now the pain had developed into a throbbing, intense headache. He'd take that over something worse.

"Fine," said Mandy, unprompted. "I'll tell you."

"It's fine," said Max. "I don't need to know."

"No, no, I can tell you want to know. It's nothing you did, really. It's just that he was trying so hard to find you. He thought you'd have it all figured out. You're his brother, and he looks up to you. Basically it's his own expectations meeting reality. And it's not your fault, Max."

"I didn't think it was."

"It's that no one can conquer all this... madness... this chaos. The EMP changed everything. I guess he was trying to find a way back to his old life in a sense. By finding you."

"How much of that did he tell you, and how much of that is your own analysis?"

"It's a mix of both."

That wasn't really what Max had asked, but he let it drop. John would learn in time to confront whatever he was going through. He'd have to face reality, like the rest of them. And the reality was that Max wasn't anyone's savior. He was just a guy who knew how to keep going.

Max's eyes hadn't stopped moving since they'd left camp. He kept his gaze shifting between the ground and the surroundings. There were footprints everywhere that made paths back to camp. What Max was looking for was a set of footprints that didn't belong.

"It's harder than I thought to distinguish between these," said Max. "It's too bad we couldn't have followed their original prints, from when they left camp. But too much snow's fallen."

"Why didn't we at least set out in the direction they did?" said Mandy.

"Not much point," said Max. "They could have gone any direction a minute or ten minutes later after leaving. We're as likely to find signs of them out here as in any direction."

"Doesn't sound like you're holding out much hope we'll find them."

"Unfortunately not," said Max.

"I don't want to go blaming them," said Mandy. "But it's kind of their fault. I mean, I feel terrible just having said that, knowing they might be dead."

"Probably dead," said Max, correcting her.

"That makes me feel even worse."

Max didn't say anything. He was trying to make sense of the footprints.

"Why are you carrying that rifle, anyway?" said Mandy, after a few minutes.

"You're asking me why I'm carrying a gun? You are too."

"Yeah, but you know how to use the semi-automatics from the dead guys. I thought they were better guns."

"Not better," said Max. "Just different. And while I may know how to use it, I feel more comfortable with one of Georgia's rifles. Sometimes the best tool is the one you know how to use the best, rather than how it looks on paper. Unfortunately, I spent too much time at the target range with my Glock, and not enough with anything else."

"Seems like you're doing fine with it."

Up ahead, Max saw something. He stopped in his tracks, and raised his binoculars to his eyes.

"What is it?" said Mandy.

"Looks like a dead animal," said Max. "But it's hard to tell. It's pretty far off. Come on."

They continued forward, through the snow, in silence. Max's finger rested outside the trigger guard of his rifle. But he was ready.

"Can you see it now?" said Mandy. She sounded nervous.

"Yeah," said Max, using the binoculars again. "I think it's a dog."

"A dead dog?" said Mandy. She sounded upset.

Soon enough, they were close enough to see the dog with the naked eye.

"Someone shot it," said Mandy, bending down to examine it. "I wonder what it was doing out here."

Max touched the dog. "It's still warm," he said.

"It's horrible," said Mandy. "Why would someone shoot a dog?"

Max didn't answer.

Max kept his eyes on the surroundings. He doubted whoever had shot the dog was still here, but he didn't want to take his chances. He used his binoculars again, but he saw nothing.

"Maybe it was the same men who attacked us," said Mandy.

"Maybe," said Max.

'You think it was someone else?"

Max didn't say anything. He was looking at the ground now, at a pair of very clean footprints that began not far from the dog.

"Where are you going?"

Max bent down, examining the prints.

"Look at these."

"Look like boot prints. It must have been those men."

"The dog wasn't shot long ago," said Max. "It means there's someone else out here. Could be more than one."

"There's only one set of footprints."

"No," said Max, pointing. "There's two."

"But what's that over there?"

Mandy walked slightly ahead of Max, pointing to a strange pattern in the snow.

"Looks like the mark a sled would make," said Mandy. "But that doesn't make sense."

"It wasn't a sled," said Max, following the strange tracks. "Take a look at this."

"What is it?"

It was a mound in the snow about the size and shape of a body.

"Give me a hand," said Max, starting to dig at the snow with his bare hands.

"I have a feeling we're not going to like what we find."

Mandy suddenly let out a gasp, standing up and backing away from the mound.

Max looked. It was Rose. Mandy had been digging by her head, and had revealed her face. Her eyes were open wide, and the color was gone from her.

Max continued digging. Whoever'd buried Rose had done so hastily. The snow wasn't packed in tightly.

"Keep an eye on our surroundings," said Max. His hands were cold and numb, but he kept digging.

It didn't take him long to reveal the whole body.

"Someone cut off her ear!" said Mandy. "I think I'm going to be sick."

Max examined the corpse, thinking he'd find a bullet wound. But there was nothing. Not until he pushed Rose over on her stomach did he find the knife wounds.

"This is my fault," said Max. "We should have left earlier."

26

CYNTHIA

John and Cynthia had left the camp twenty minutes ago. Cynthia was exhausted from the night before, and annoyed that no one else was complaining about it much.

John had been acting strangely since they'd left. Cynthia could almost felt his anger. And she knew it wasn't about the battle last night. And it wasn't about fearing for their lives. It was something that wasn't quite about survival.

"I don't see how we can just go, go, go," said Cynthia. "Don't you realize that people need to rest?"

"We're looking for two missing members of our group," snapped John. "Don't you think that's a little more important than you getting your beauty sleep?"

"Beauty sleep? When's the last time we slept at all? Who said anything about looking good?"

"Sorry," said John. "I know you're tired. So am I."

"And I know we need to look for Jake and Rose," said Cynthia. "It's just you're not making this easy. What's going on with you, anyway?"

"It's nothing," said John.

"It's your brother, isn't it?"

John didn't answer.

"Come on, John. Why don't you talk to me about it?"

John muttered something unintelligible.

"Yeah, I know. Men don't like to talk about their feelings." Cynthia add her classic sarcastic bite to her words. That usually got John to talk, even when he was being too quiet for her liking.

"It's not that," said John. "It's just there's no point in talking about it."

"What? Talking doesn't fix anything? Sounds like a typical male answer."

"No," said John. "Like I said, it's not that."

"Then what is it?"

"Max is right. There are more important things at stake right now than how I feel about... certain things."

"You mean your brother?"

John didn't answer.

"I know you're disappointed," said Cynthia.

"What? How?"

"Women's intuition."

"Mandy told you?"

"Maybe," said Cynthia, not wanting to fully reveal her sources. "Look, what you're feeling is normal."

"How so? What do you know about it?"

"There's no reason to get upset with me," snapped Cynthia.

"I'm not," said John.

But it was clear that he was.

"You were hoping Max would be something like our savior. I mean, you and I talked about it enough. You can't pretend that isn't the case."

"OK," snapped John. "So what if it was?"

Cynthia glanced at John. She'd rarely seen him like this, so upset and angry. She'd touched a nerve. Together, they'd been through countless trials, many near-death situations. There'd been many times where they'd thought they'd never make it out alive. And yet, she'd never seen this anger in him before. Not like this. It was different. More personal.

Cynthia had the instinct to back off of the topic, to let sleeping dogs lie. But, for some reason, she continued. "I just don't get what you're upset about. Max is great. I mean, without him, we'd definitely be dead."

"Oh, is that so?" said John. "Well you don't know what you're talking about. You don't have any idea."

He spoke to her in angry, aggressive tones, and his eyes glared at her.

Cynthia shivered, recoiling from the expression his face.

"What's gotten into you?" she said.

"Nothing. Nothing's gotten into me. I'm fine."

But he was visibly angry. His body was quivering, almost shaking with anger.

"If this is all about Max, then I think the best thing to do is..."

"Just shut up, would you?" snapped John.

It had come on all of a sudden, this mood, and it surprised Cynthia. She'd thought she'd known John. She'd thought what they'd been through together had let her know him as well as anyone could. But there were always dark parts of a person, things that rarely revealed themselves. And when they did, they were shocking.

"I've never seen you like this," said Cynthia. "Why

don't you take a couple deep breaths. You need to calm down."

"I don't need to do anything!" shouted John, screaming right in her face.

"What the hell?" said Cynthia. "Don't scream at me, damnit."

"Why don't you just head back to camp?" said John, his eyes burning with anger. "I can do this on my own. I don't need you, or anyone else. I don't need Max."

"Look, I'm sorry, I guess I touched some nerve about your childhood... I thought..."

"You've said all you need to. I'm doing this alone."

John picked up his pace, nearly breaking into a run.

Cynthia tried to keep up, but his legs were longer than hers. And she was already having trouble walking through the snow.

"John, wait up!"

John didn't look back. He was already many paces ahead of her.

"We're supposed to go together! There are dangerous people out here!"

"There's no one out here," shouted John, without turning around.

It was the last thing he said to her.

She couldn't keep up. Her legs were already burning, trying to run through the snow. The rifle felt heavy in her hands, impossibly heavy.

It wasn't just the physical sensation that slowed her down. It was the knowledge that since she'd known John, he'd never once abandoned her. It wasn't like him to leave her on her own out in the woods, out in the dangerous wilds, where anyone could come along at any moment.

She was all alone. John had disappeared into the trees.

"Shit," muttered Cynthia, sitting down in the snow.

It had all happened so fast. She felt hurt and betrayed. John had never run off like that before, leaving her there on her own. Not if he could help it. No, before he'd done everything in his power to be there for her, to protect her as best he could, even when they were compete strangers and he'd had no reason to.

It was that childhood stuff. Old wounds and all that. Maybe he had his reason to be upset.

But he should be upset with Max, not Cynthia. She didn't have anything to do with it. And even on the Max front, it didn't really make sense. From what Cynthia could tell, Max was a good guy. He was always helping the rest of them. He was always going out of his way to push himself trying to protect the others. And for what? For nothing. He didn't ask for anything in return, except that the others be vigilant and cautious. Not to mention smart about what they were doing.

Max certainly wouldn't have approved of John going off on his own, leaving Cynthia there.

An eerie feeling crept over Cynthia. She looked around at the snow and the snow-covered trees, shivering in the cold, and realized quite viscerally that she was completely alone.

Or so she hoped.

Max had been convinced there were others out there. John didn't think so, but maybe whatever problem he had with his brother was blinding him to the truth.

Cynthia felt not just alone, but exposed. Despite all her practice with firearms, she didn't feel confident. Sure, she'd fought before. She'd survived. But that was then. Each new situation brought new dangers.

What was she supposed to do? Should she head back to camp, finding protection among the others there?

But what about John? He was out on his own, apparently confident that there was no danger now, that everything was fine.

It just didn't make sense. If there was anything John and Cynthia had learned together, it was that nothing was ever fine, and that new dangers lurked around every corner, every tree. Each passing minute and hour had always, so far, meant new threats on their life.

John might need her. Cynthia wasn't mad at him. Sure, he'd blown up at her. But that could be forgiven. She had to remember all the other times, the times he'd saved her from certain death, the times he'd been kind to her when he hadn't needed to. These were stressful situations of the worst kind. People could be excused for having a blow up now and again.

But what couldn't be forgiven was leaving her. Striking out on his own. Potentially it meant as much danger as it did for her as it did for him.

Cynthia made her up her mind. She wasn't going to leave John out there on his own. He couldn't keep up that pace for long, running through the snow like that. He'd have to slow down.

All she had to do was follow his tracks.

Cynthia stood up, took a deep breath, and headed in the direction John had disappeared in.

27

SADIE

"Do you think this is ever going to end, Mom?" said Sadie.

"What's going to end?"

"All this. The violence. Everything that's happened..." Sadie didn't quite know how to express what she was trying to say. It felt like they had been going and going, with hardly any breaks, any time to think. This was one of the few moments of peace they'd had over the last weeks.

And it wasn't even really peace. After all, Jake and Rose were missing. Max and the others were out looking for them. Max was convinced there were other bad guys out there. And if Sadie had learned anything since the EMP, it was that Max was often right. Not always. But a lot of the time.

Her mother was silent for a long time, continuing to scan the surroundings, her rifle by her side.

"I don't know how to explain it," continued Sadie. "I feel like I should have learned this in English class or something. But I don't..."

"Sadie," said her mother, speaking slowly and with

sadness in her voice. "This is too much for someone your age to have to go through. It's not surprising that you don't have the words to say what you're trying to say."

Sadie thought for a moment, then said, "I don't think anyone should have to go through this. No matter how old."

Her mother chuckled. "Maybe you're right, Sadie. But I guess this is what we get."

"What do you mean?"

"Well, I don't know if we deserve it. I wouldn't go that far. But our whole society... it was foolish in a lot of ways."

"Like everyone not knowing how to shoot, use a gun, hunt deer like you do?"

"That's part of it. But think about this... where did all our food come from when we were living in the suburbs?"

"Well, you shot a lot of deer."

Georgia chuckled again. "Yes, but that's not all we ate. In fact, I bet it didn't make up more than 10% of our calories. Where'd the rest come from?"

"The grocery store."

"Yeah, but where'd it come from before that?"

Sadie shrugged her shoulders. "I don't know."

"It came from all over. On trucks, right? You've seen them behind the store, unloading."

Sadie nodded her head.

"Food came from all over. Damn, it's weird to talk about this in the past tense. Anyway, they'd ship food to us from all over the world. And the whole country was run like that. Think about it, Sadie, it could have come from ten minutes away, if the infrastructure had been set up like that."

"But where would people have grown it? It's not like

there are any farms around or anything. None that I've seen."

"Well, you remember out by Valley Forge? That whole area used to be farmland. Gradually, the farmers sold it off to developers. That's where all those houses came from. Just a way for someone to get really rich. Not that I blame them, necessarily. They were just looking out for their own families. Maybe I would have done the same thing, but it didn't work out too well for us."

"But Mom," said Sadie. "How would that have helped us? We had to get out. We had to leave. Max said we would have been killed if we'd stayed."

"You're probably right, Sadie," said Georgia, sighing. "I guess there's not much point in philosophizing about it anyway. It's all a moot point now."

"I hope Max and Mandy are OK," said Sadie, shivering slightly as she stared out at the snow-covered landscape. "At least it's a little warmer now, I guess."

"They'll be fine," said Georgia. "They know how to take care of themselves. John and Cynthia, too. They did well last night."

"I don't think they could have done it without you, though."

Georgia laughed. "I'm not doing much good now."

"That's crazy, Mom. You're the best shot of any of them, and you're walking a lot better now."

"You know me, Sadie. It's hard for me to sit back and let others do things for me. Remember our house? I mean, when did I ever hire a plumber or a painter?"

"You wouldn't even hire an electrician! You almost got electrocuted."

Georgia laughed. "Yeah, that probably would have been better done by a professional."

"And James convinced you to hire a plumber once, when he'd clogged up the toilet really badly. You finally caved in, and then you made the poor guy's life impossible. You wouldn't let him work."

"I did too!"

"By standing behind him and telling him he was doing it all wrong?"

"Well, he was! He didn't know what he was doing."

"Then why didn't you do it?"

"Maybe you have a point, Sadie," said Georgia, a grin on her face. "Wow, it feels good to laugh. It's been a while. Too long."

"I guess that's what I was trying to explain earlier," said Sadie. "Everything's been so, I don't know, serious. Intense. There isn't any time to live, really. I mean, I can do without my cell phone."

"James would argue differently."

"I'm getting used to it! I've hardly even looked at in the last week."

"You're not still hoping it'll turn back on?"

"I know it won't. It's just a habit, I guess, looking it. It used to be a sort of comforting thing. And I never even realized it until it didn't work anymore. But what I was saying is I can live without all the comforts we had. You know what I mean, like food in the fridge, a bed to sleep in, stuff like that. But it's the other stuff, like feeling like we're constantly in danger. Like we could die at any moment. Or like I could lose you or James."

"That's not going to happen, Sadie," said Georgia, putting her arm around her daughter.

"I hope not."

28

MARSHAL

The thrill of his last kill was still with him. It was so much better doing it himself than simply watching and listening to men dying. Completely different. No comparison.

Killing that dog hadn't done it for him. He'd killed so many animals that it was merely a matter of routine. There wasn't that thrill. That spark.

He knew he wouldn't be able to wait long. The plan had been to wait patiently. To bide his time. To pick them off one by one.

Sure, he was still going to do that. He'd be careful. But he needed another one. Another kill. Just one more, then he'd hide again and wait. Well, maybe two more. Depended on how things went. He'd have to wait and see. If the opportunity was there, he wouldn't pass it up.

This time was going to be different. He was working on a plan. He'd do it at his leisure this time, with no fear of interruptions. The woods were big, and there were a lot of places to hide. A lot of places to do what he needed to do.

Marshal wasn't that far from the camp. After killing that woman, he'd taken a path that ran around the camp in a large half-circle. His plan was to get to the other side. After that, he didn't know. He needed more to his plan. He needed to think. He needed to speed up a little.

Marshal had been taking amphetamines the entire journey, ever since leaving the militia boundaries. He'd been doling them out to himself, one by one, about every four hours or so. They were time release tablets, white and plain looking. A protective coating around the outside of the tablet slowed the tablet's breakdown in the stomach, roughing the rate at which the drug entered his system.

But Marshal needed something more. He sat down behind a tree, propped his gun up, and took out the orange plastic prescription bottle. Opening the safety cap, Marshal shook out two pills. He needed a good kick.

Swallowing the pills wasn't going to do it for him.

From his pocket, Marshal took out a small gift card, the type of card that had always been floating around the prison. It no longer had any value on it, not that that mattered now, but at one point it had. They'd been a sort of unofficial currency in the prison, the way packs of cigarettes often were.

It was a little strange taking the card out and looking at it. The name of the store was plastered in bright colors across the front of the hard, rigid plastic. The name meant nothing now. And it never would again.

Marshal liked the card because of its stiffness. So often the gift cards he'd seen were that filmy type of plastic. Not any good for snorting.

Resting the card on his knee, Marshal place the tablets carefully on top. Using the butt of his survival knife,

Marshal crushed and ground the pills into a fine off-white powder.

Leaning down, his nose near his knee, Marshal pressed his index finger against the outside of his nose, blocking off one nostril. With the other, he inhaled deeply, the powder burning his nose all the way up his sinuses. He enjoyed the harsh, burning feeling.

The effect was almost instantaneous. He was already starting to feel it as he switched nostrils and inhaled again, sharply and deeply.

The effect was one not just of energy. But of power, raw and cold. He felt physically capable of almost anything, with a cold adrenaline-like energy rushing through his body. His mind was sharper and swifter than usual.

He felt cold and calculating, just the way he liked it.

Finished with his powder, Marshal was renewed. Not just refreshed, but stronger than before.

Marshal stood up, breathing in deeply, tucking the gift card carefully back into his pocket.

When he grabbed his gun, he knew the sound.

Footsteps coming from the direction of the camp.

Marshal waited, listening carefully. He heard no voices. Just one person slogging through the snow.

Marshal could barely believe his luck. It was like someone was being delivered to him. A new victim, a new set of thrills and pleasure.

Marshal already knew the plan.

It was simple. Easy. And foolproof.

Nothing could go wrong.

A single, narrow trail led through the trees. It was almost a completely certainty that whoever it was would come down this trail. Marshal didn't have to do any guesswork.

Marshal got into position, rushing over to a tree near the trail. It was a large pine tree, with long drooping branches that would give him the complete cover and secrecy he needed.

Now he waited. Like a spider, lying in wait. The only difference between himself and the spider was that he himself was the trap. Just him and his gun. And his cunning.

The spider killed for food. Marshal was fulfilling a similarly crucial need. To kill. To cause pain.

The footsteps were louder. They were the only sound in the area. Nothing else for miles around. No animals sounds. No chirping or squeaking. No distractions.

Marshal had to resist peeking at his prey. He was going to do this completely blind. That was the only way there'd be no risk.

He waited until the footsteps had reached him.

Marshal counted to himself slowly.

One.

Two.

Three.

Four.

Marshal knew from experience this was the perfect distance.

He stepped out from under and behind the pine tree.

His gun was aimed perfectly before he spoke.

"Don't move a muscle. Stay right where you are. Or I kill you right here and now. A bullet right in the back of the head. Not a bad way to die, but not what I'd recommend, personally."

Marshal stood behind the man. His eyes traveled up

and down the man. He was wearing one of the parkas recovered from the compound men. He carried one of their guns, too. He didn't wear a pack. He was fairly tall. His hair was overgrown and greasy, just like everyone's now.

"What do you want?"

"You're doing good so far," said Marshal. "I was worried I was going to have to shoot you."

Marshal always seemed to know what to say to convince people to do what he wanted. Sometimes he couldn't help but marvel at his own abilities. The words just seemed to tumble out of his mouth.

If the man decided to fight, Marshal would have no choice but to shoot him, injuring him and possibly killing him. That would take most of the fun away. Marshal wanted this one to be special. He wanted to take his time, starting with the most mild pain and slowly working his way up over the course of a day until finally he'd kill him.

The man was breathing heavily. Marshal saw his arm starting to move ever so slightly, just barely twitching. If Marshal didn't say just the right thing, the guy was going to go for his gun.

"Look," said Marshal, using his most sympathetic tones. "I don't want to do this. You've got to understand me. But I'm desperate. I don't have any food, and I'm exhausted and hungry, basically at the end of my rope."

The man said nothing.

Marshal knew he had to appear sympathetic in order to get this man to drop his weapons. Marshal was too careful to approach him now to try to tie him up. Marshal would probably end up being attacked.

The man was on the brink of trying to attack Marshal, probably knowing full well he was going to get shot. But all Marshal had to do was convince him he wouldn't hurt him. He had to make the decision easy.

"What's your name?" said Marshal.

"John," said the man after a long pause.

"Look, John," said Marshal. "Trust me, I'm not this kind of person. I was an accountant before the blackout, before everything went to shit. Imagine that, just a little office worker who was good at keeping his head down during lay-offs, suddenly out on his own, starving in the wilderness."

John didn't say anything.

"I was doing OK, but now I'm literally about to die from hunger. And I've got a kid to look after. If it was just me, hell, I'd just let myself starve to death. You get what I'm saying, right?"

"Maybe," said John, speaking slowly.

"I know there's a camp out here with plenty of food. I need some of that food. For my kid. I don't want to hurt anyone. And I can't risk going to that camp. I know how people are now. I know what this blackout has done to humanity. Everyone's an animal now. Not me, though. I mean, I will if I have to. I'll act like that for my kid."

John didn't say anything.

"We're all in this together," said Marshal. "I don't want to hurt you. I really don't. It's the last thing I want to do."

"Then why are you doing this?"

"Look, I'm just going to take you hostage. You'll be my bargaining chip with your friends at the camp. They'll give me the food I need, and I'll return you. No one gets hurt. It's easy. Then I'll move on out of here and everything will be fine."

"They won't hurt you," said John. "At the camp, I mean. I know them. If you really have a kid…"

"Of course I do!"

"We'd never hurt a kid," said John. "And new people are always joining the group. If you're a good person, they'll help you out, or even take you in."

"I heard gunshots last night," said Marshal. "I don't trust people like that. I don't think you're who you say you are."

"We were attacked," said John. "You'd have done the exact same thing. Our lives were on the line. But if you come in peace, it'd be completely different. And the way to start that is to put down your gun and let me turn around."

"I'm afraid that's not going to happen," said Marshal. "So put your guns down, or I'll be forced to shoot you."

"How are you going to use me as a bargaining chip if you shoot me?"

"Like I said, I don't want to shoot you. But I will. I'm a desperate man."

John breathed out heavily, and slowly placed his gun on the ground.

"Now the handgun," said Marshal. "And no tricks either."

John removed his handgun from its holster and placed it on the ground.

"And the knife," said Marshal.

John took two knives out, one folding and one fixed blade, and placed them next to the guns.

"Now take five long, slow steps forward."

John did as Marshal asked.

Marshal was starting to feel it. He was close to his goal. So close.

Marshal had already taken the rope he'd brought along out of his pack, having slung it around his shoulder.

He pulled at it now, took out his knife, and cut off a length of it that he used to bind John's wrists tightly together. Marshal wasn't taking any chances. He pulled as hard as he could, doubling and then tripling the knot. Marshal did it from the front, wanting to savor the budding expression of hopelessness on John's face.

"Can you still feel your hands?"

"Yeah," said John.

"Good," said Marshal. "I want you to feel everything."

"Feel everything?"

"You'll see," said Marshal.

Marshal started to bend down, ready to bind John's legs together. But as he did so, John made his move, swinging his bound arms together, like a pendulum that came right at Marshal's head.

Marshal was too fast for him. He ducked easily, then threw himself forwards, knocking John to the ground.

Their bodies fell together into the snow. John brought both arms up, his hands in fist, slamming them into Marshal's stomach.

Marshal grunted in pain.

Then he grinned.

It just made it all the more thrilling.

Marshal brought his right fist up high, slamming it down into John's face. It hit him in the nose. He probably broke it. Blood gushed down John's face.

Marshal had his handgun out, and jammed it with one hand into John's mouth, forcing his lips open. With his other hand, he gripped John's neck tightly, applying just the right amount of pressure.

"Now you're going to cooperate," said Marshal. "And I don't need to give you my reasons."

John's eyes were wild looking. The fight hadn't left him. Not yet.

The amphetamines were still in full effect. Marshal almost had to struggle against them, against the violent exuberant energy that coursed through him. He had to hold back. He couldn't simply kill John here and now. He needed to be patient, to wait. That was the only way he could get the full effect, the full joy of the experience.

John was troublesome. He'd fight. He wouldn't let himself go easily. Now he seemed to understand that Marshal hadn't been telling the truth. Maybe he'd guessed it all along. But it didn't matter since he'd allowed himself to at least partially believe it, relaxing enough for Marshal to make his move.

Marshal couldn't figure out how to tie up John without risking his own life. John was clearly ready to fight. He'd been hoping to drag John away fully conscious. That way John could appreciate what was going to happen to himself. He'd be aware of every moment, of every moment of pain that was fast approaching. Marshal would explain it to him all on the trip as he dragged John's fully-bound body through the snow like a sled.

But he'd have to compromise. At least this compromise wasn't as bad as the last one Marshal had killed.

And he could still have some fun, even in the little things, the tricks he loved to play.

"OK," said Marshal. "I guess you're right. I'm sorry. I'll untie you."

John's eyes flickered with confusion.

"Look," said Marshal. "I'm not going to shoot you. I'll even untie you. Just don't hurt me."

Marshal removed the handgun from John's mouth.

Marshal could see it in John's eyes. John was about to attack. He was just waiting for the right moment.

Marshal brought the pistol up high.

John lunged up and forward, shoving himself against Marshal.

Flipping the gun in his hand, Marshal brought the butt of it down hard against the side of John's skull. Hard enough to knock him out. Not hard enough to kill him.

Marshal sprung into action. He cut another section of rope, and tied John's legs together tightly, at his ankles and also right below his knees. He also tied his arms together right below the elbows.

Marshal was in the process of figuring out the best way to rig John up like a sled so that he could drag him through the snow when off in the distance he saw a lone figure approaching.

Another victim. Just what he needed.

He just had to be careful. He didn't want to kill whoever it was too early.

29

CYNTHIA

There was someone off in the distance, waving at her. He was wearing a parka, just like the one she was wearing.

It didn't look like John. But it was hard to tell. For years now, her eyesight had always gotten significantly worse when she'd been tired, even though she didn't wear glasses. Her doctor had told her it was normal.

She was definitely tired now. Exhausted beyond the point she'd thought she could stand.

Looking through the scope of her rifle, she saw his face. It wasn't John.

Cynthia moved the gun. There was something on the ground.

A body.

Was it John?

He must have come this way. This was where his footprints led.

Max had been right. There'd been more out there.

Cynthia felt the panic rising through her.

Was John dead?

The man in the parka was furiously waving his arms in the air, signaling for help. He didn't seem to have a gun.

Maybe he was someone else. Maybe he wasn't an enemy. Maybe something had happened to John, and this man was trying to help.

She shouldn't take any chances. She couldn't afford to. It was life and death out here.

The feelings she had for John suddenly came to the surface, only causing her to panic more. She cared about him. Deeply. If he was still alive, she needed to do something.

"Don't move!" shouted Cynthia, as loudly as she could.

The man kept waving his hands.

The man was shouting something. Very loudly. But they were far away. She could only make out some of the words. It sounded like he was saying "hurt!" or something similar.

Maybe the safest thing to do was just shoot the man dead. Maybe that'd be the best thing not just for herself, but for John's chances of survival as well.

Then again, if John was hurt and not dead, the situation was completely different. There was no one else around. There was no way to contact anyone at the camp for help. Max and Mandy had gone in the opposite direction.

Cynthia crept forward, using her scope to keep an eye on the situation.

She realized that she might not have been thinking clearly due to exhaustion, due to fatigue, due to extreme stress. Her emotions were running wild, and she couldn't keep them in check. Deep breaths were doing nothing. Her pulse was skyrocketing. She felt like she was hyperventilating.

She and John had been through so much. She'd seen so many deaths. She'd seen her husband gunned down in front of her. She'd seen more bodies than she'd ever thought possible. More blood. More guts. Even brains. Dead animals. She lived now in the woods, carried a gun daily, and hadn't showered in who knew how long. Her body had tightened up. She'd lost weight and some muscle. She thought she'd toughened up. She thought she could deal with a situation like this.

She'd seen John injured before, when she hadn't known if he'd make it. She'd seen him on the brink of death.

In those situations, she'd kept as calm a head as she could.

What was different now?

Maybe nothing. Maybe it was just hard, if not impossible, to remember what she'd really been feeling in those situations. Maybe her memory had tricked her, telling her that she'd dealt with those situations fine. It could be a sort of survival mechanism.

But it wasn't doing her any good now. This felt like the first time she was experiencing all this.

Her boots crunched in the snow as she slowly inched forward.

The man standing didn't move except to wave his hands.

"He's hurt!" he was shouting. His words were becoming more clear the closer Cynthia got.

They were close enough now to have a conversation by shouting at each other. Cynthia used the scope on her rifle to scan the area, looking for weapons. There were none, except for John's gun, which lay partially buried in the snow. The stranger didn't make a move for it. He didn't look threatening. There was an honest expression on his face. Not that his expression meant anything.

"What happened?" shouted Cynthia.

"He fell. Must have slipped. He's unconscious. I just found him like this."

Cynthia was frozen, gun in her hands, eye pressed to the scope. She didn't know what to do.

"Come on! I need help. I'm not going to hurt you."

There was a genuine quality to the stranger's voice. It made her want to trust him.

Every part of her wanted to trust him. It would be easier that way. After all, everyone couldn't be bad. Right? Just because the EMP had hit and society had collapsed, it didn't mean that everyone suddenly turned into some kind of monster. Right? That'd be impossible.

Cynthia remembered that not that long ago, John had been a stranger himself. And he wasn't a monster. He wasn't a cold-hearted killer. He was a good man. And so was Max. And there was Georgia, Mandy, and many others. They'd been good people. Surely there were other good people out there.

"I was going to try to drag him to my camp," the man was shouting. "That's why I've got him tied up like this. I couldn't wake him up no matter what I tried. I didn't know what to do."

That part of the story checked out. There was a rope trailing from John's body, just the way Cynthia would have done it if she'd needed to drag an unconscious person across the snow.

"Come on! We don't have much time. He looks really hurt. Do you have any medical training?"

Cynthia wanted to believe. She was dying to believe the stranger. And maybe she'd die for it.

She walked towards him, slowly. She slung the gun over her shoulder, and drew her handgun. She felt more comfortable with it. She kept it aimed at the stranger, who kept his hands in the air.

Finally, after what had felt like an eternity, she was there, standing mere feet away from John and the stranger.

The stranger had a kind face, flooded with concern. There was something odd about it. But she couldn't place what it was. Something incredibly minor. Something that didn't matter. Not now.

She could feel herself making up her mind. John looked like he was in bad shape. She needed to help him. She needed to trust this stranger. It might be the only way that John would survive.

It wasn't until Cynthia was very close that she noticed something strange about the way John was tied up. His legs were bound together, as if he was a prisoner.

Cynthia acted rather than spoke.

But the stranger was already moving towards her. He was fast and strong, moving like lightning, quickly closing the gap between them.

Cynthia squeezed the trigger. There wasn't time to aim properly. She did the best she could.

The stranger grunted in pain. She'd hit him.

But he kept coming. He was simply too fast.

He was tall, appearing massive in his white parka. His expression seemed to have changed. The last thing Cynthia registered was the realization that the stranger had been acting. The whole thing had been a ruse, from his voice right down to his facial expression.

His face now only showed intensity and cruelty. His face was so close to hers. Everything happened so fast.

He was swinging something at her, right at her head.

The gunshot hadn't seemed to affect him. It hadn't slowed him down.

Something hard collided with Cynthia's head. It knocked her out cold immediately.

30

JOHN

John woke up with searing pain rushing through his throbbing skull. His body felt stiff with the cold. He could barely think, let alone think straight, with his throbbing headache. It was worse than the one migraine he'd had in his life, and that migraine had kept him out of work for two days.

John tried to move. But he couldn't. His body was responding, but his legs and arms seemed to be tied together. He strained against his bindings, but it was absolutely no use. He couldn't move an inch.

He lay on his back. The ground was uneven and cold. Slowly, he opened his eyes. He was staring straight up to the sky. He could see some naked tree branches stretched out over the sky. The sky itself was cloudy and grey.

Where was he?

What had happened?

He tried to think. Where had he been last? What had been doing?

The last thing he could remember was leaving the camp early in the morning. The light had been just rising.

Or so he thought. The memory was fuzzy. His whole brain felt hazy, and he felt nauseous and dizzy. His thinking wasn't clear. It was hard to hold onto one thought for too long.

What had he been thinking about? Oh yeah, he'd been trying to remember what had happened to him, trying to figure out why he was bound and lying on the ground.

He'd left with someone. There'd been someone else, someone he cared about. He tried to get his brain to focus, to remember, but it was like trying to run that last mile of a marathon.

Suddenly, it came to him. Cynthia had been with him.

Where was she now? And what had happened in the meantime?

John knew he needed to act rationally. Even if he couldn't think rationally, he could still do something. He'd been complaining, and perhaps hurt, thinking that his brother Max didn't have the answers. But in the last week he had learned something important from Max, which was that no matter what, there was always something helpful to do, some action that would get you to a better place than when you started. No matter how hopeless things seemed, there was always something to do, something to try.

Not that John could really think thoughts like that now, remembering what his brother had told him. Instead, it was an attitude that he'd internalized over time.

It hurt immensely, but John managed to turn his head to the side, so that his cheek was pressed into the snow.

There was a man not far away. Only a few feet. He seemed familiar but John couldn't place him.

He opened his eyes wider, trying to see, even though the extra light only seemed to make the pain worse.

"Ah, you're awake. Good." The man spoke in a strange way, with a strange cadence.

"Who are you?" said John. His voice came out scratch and raspy. How long had he been unconscious? Maybe he was dehydrated. Just speaking those words made the pain in his head worse.

"Who am I? That's a complicated question to ask anyone. I mean, who are any of us?"

It took John a moment to process this strange reply.

"No, I mean. Who are you? And why do you have me tied up like this?"

"You mean you don't remember me?"

"No," said John, the words causing him more pain.

The stranger had been facing slightly away from John. Now he turned fully towards him. He wasn't wearing a jacket, and one of his shirt sleeves was missing. It looked like it'd been cut off. Bits of frayed cloth hung down.

The man had some kind of wound, right below his shoulder, where a tape bandage covered the flesh.

John was so cold it was hard to imagine that the stranger could stand the temperatures without a jacket.

"Well this is a strange development," said the stranger. "This is going to... ruin it a little for me..."

"What? Ruin what?"

"I'll have to explain everything to you, I suppose. Otherwise, you won't understand what's going on. Who knows how badly I damaged your brain. I wouldn't worry about it, though. You won't need it for much longer. The principal thing is that you can get the idea into your head that I'm about to torture you. It's going to be painful. As painful as I can possibly make it. I want you to fully understand that fact. Otherwise, you'll just be some incoherent mess of pain. And that doesn't really do it for me. Not at all."

John's confused mind was reeling. He understood everything well enough to know he'd soon die.

Unless he could find a way out.

He thrashed against his bindings. But it accomplished nothing. Nothing at all.

Cynthia.

He'd left with Cynthia.

Where was she?

"Where is she?" said John.

"Your friend? She tried to save you. But I tricked her, and she didn't realize what was going on until it was too late. You're all the same, all of you. Your feeble minds are so easily fooled by a sign of faked emotion. I just don't understand it. And I never will."

John watched as the man snorted something from a small plastic card. Maybe it was a credit card, nothing but a relic of the pre-EMP world.

"Don't worry about this little injury," said the demented stranger. "Your friend tried her best, like I said. It was worth it to me to receive this injury, if the trade-off was going to be that she lived. At least for a little while. This won't slow me down. Not in the least bit."

So Cynthia was alive.

"Where do you have her? Where is she?"

"Where is she? Are you blind? She's right behind you. So you two care about each other, is that right? What is it? Something romantic? A husband-wife situation? Girlfriend-boyfriend? That'll make this all the better. You'll be in pain when I hurt her, and vice-versa. I knew she cared enough about you to try to help you, but that could happen between strangers. You're all so boring, all you normal people, and yet so interesting."

John turned his head over, facing the other direction. It caused him considerable pain to do so. Something wasn't right about his neck, or his back.

Cynthia was there, tied up just like he was. She was unconscious.

"Cynthia," hissed John. "Cynthia, wake up."

But she didn't wake up. He could see she was still breathing, though. She was still alive. For now.

"Don't worry, she'll wake up eventually. She'll be able to see what I do to you. You know, I was going to wait until you were both awake. For the full effect. But I think I'll start off slow with you, and see if your screams wake her up. This is going to take a while, anyway, and there's plenty of time for fun with the both of you."

The man, still not wearing a jacket, drew a large knife from somewhere. He stood up and began walking towards John.

John thrashed again against the rope that bound him. But it was no use. There was nothing he could do. He was helpless. The helplessness itself ate away at him, causing him deep emotional pain.

If he could have only done something. If he could have only gone down fighting. That would have been better. Far better.

"Let's start with the fingernails, shall we?" said the stranger, leaning down over John. He laughed. "No, we'll move onto that. First thing's first, let's see some blood. Just a little. Don't worry, I'm not going to let you bleed out. The end will be much more painful than that."

The man moved out of view. John felt him tugging on his pant leg, doing something with it. He heard the sounds of fabric tearing. John felt the cold of the snow and the air against his now-bare leg. The man had cut away part of his pants, from the knee downward.

John felt the knife running delicately across his skin. The steel was cold, but it didn't yet cut him or pierce him.

A second later, that changed.

John barely felt it, but he knew the knife had cut him.

"Like I said," said the stranger. "I like to start off slow. This is the lowest amount of pain you'll feel for the rest of the day. Soon enough I'll break out the pliers. I always have them with me. You know, so I can remove your nails."

31

MAX

Max and Mandy had followed the footprints in the snow for a long time.

"It looks like he's walking fast. Very fast," said Max.

"How can you tell?"

"It's just a guess based on how far apart the prints are. And think about how warm the body was. We're moving at a good pace, but he's still ahead of us. By a lot."

"Take a look at that."

Up ahead, the snow had been greatly disturbed. There were clusters of footprints in one area as well as a place, about the size of a body, where the snow had been pushed aside.

"What the hell happened here?" said Mandy, when they got to the area. She bent down, trying to get a closer look at the prints and strange marks.

Max said nothing for a moment. His gaze was off in the distance, trying to make sense of the various paths.

"There's blood," said Mandy.

"Something happened here," said Max.

"What, though?"

"Don't know. But someone's in trouble."

"Don't you think they're already dead?"

"There's no body. And look at those tracks. Looks like someone dragged a body through the snow."

"Maybe they were just trying to hide it?"

"Maybe."

"It could be anyone," said Mandy. "It could have been Georgia, John..."

"No point in worry about it," said Max, cutting her off. "There's no way to contact them to see what happened. The only thing to do is follow the tracks, and deal with the situation once we get there."

"What if we can't?"

"Can't?"

"I mean what if we can't deal with it. Whoever this is has already killed once. Probably twice."

"We have to try," said Max.

He was already leading the way, walking through the snow. A gust of wind blew in, chilling his face. The wind cut through his pants. The cold seemed to make his leg hurt more.

They walked quickly, side by side when they could, following the path. It was clear and easy to follow.

"It looks like they were dragging something else," said Mandy.

Max nodded. "That's what I was thinking."

"You think it's John and Cynthia? They were supposed to be over in that area."

"Could be," said Max.

They were already going as fast as they could. There wasn't any point in running. It would just tire them out more.

Mandy kept glancing at Max as they walked, apparently trying to read something from his expression. But Max's face remained impassive.

They had walked for another half an hour when Mandy's boot caught against something in the snow. She tripped, falling forward, before Max could catch her.

"You all right?" he said, bending down to help her.

"Yeah," she said, wincing in pain. "I'm fine."

"What hurts?"

"My ankle."

"Let's see if you can put weight on it."

Max helped her to her feet, but when she tried to support her own weight, she simply couldn't. She grunted in pain, trying not to let out her scream.

"It's bad," said Max.

"No shit," said Mandy, gritting her teeth.

"You're not going to be able to walk on that."

"You go on ahead," said Mandy, looking him dead in the eyes. "They might be alive. They need you."

Max gave her a stiff nod. "I'll get you propped up against this tree here. Keep your gun ready. Keep your eyes open, and stay alert, no matter how bad the pain is."

"It's not that bad. I'll be fine."

But Max had to basically carry her to the tree.

"If I don't make it back," said Max. "Make a set of crutches and get back to camp."

"Don't talk like that. You're going to make it back."

"Stay alert," said Max.

Then he was off, walking as fast as he could through the snow, following the tracks.

In another fifteen minutes, he was there. He saw no one. Not yet. But he heard a voice, loud. It sounded like someone was ranting. A man's voice.

Max decided to cut around the side, circling the area, so that he wouldn't arrive from the same direction that the man had. That way he could hope to have the element of surprise more on his side.

Max made his way through the snow and the trees, trying to keep behind the trees as much as possible.

The voice continued. Max could hear it more clearly now. He was closer. He didn't stop to look through his scope. He wanted to act as quickly as possible.

Max flattened himself behind a tree, finger on the trigger. He was ready. He was breathing heavily. His leg throbbed.

"I'm giving you a break. Now that the both of you are awake, it's going to be a lot more interesting. I don't want to overwhelm you. At least not yet. There's plenty of time for that. No one's going to find us here." It was definitely a man's voice, loud and powerful.

"Why don't you just let her go? You can do what you want with me." It was Max's brother's voice.

"No! John!" It was Cynthia's voice.

"Don't worry, lady. I'd never pass up the opportunity to torture both of you to death. I'm not letting your boyfriend go."

There was silence for a long moment. Then a scream. Cynthia's. Loud, filled with pain. It pierced the silence of the woods, reverberating in Max's brain. He had to act. Fast. Who knew how long John and Cynthia had.

Max moved out from behind the tree. His rifle was ready. The area was in his scope.

A man was standing over two bodies on the ground.

Max pulled the trigger.

The rifle kicked back.

The man moved. Going for a gun. Fast.

Max had missed.

Max threw himself back behind the tree just in time. Bullets slammed into the trunk. It was last night all over again.

"Who's out there? Who's come to play?"

Max thought for a moment. Should he answer?

Max didn't know who he was dealing with. Except that they were dangerous. And an indiscriminate killer.

Max moved again, out from behind the tree. He was ready, his eye to the scope. But the stranger wasn't there.

On instinct, Max got behind the tree again, rather than looking for the stranger.

Another blast of gunfire. Bullets thudded into the tree.

Max was breathing heavily. Sweat dripped down his brow despite the temperature. One of his boots had dug into the dirt underneath the snow.

"You can't beat me!" shouted the stranger. There was a strange quality to his voice. Taunting, but cold and emotionless. Yet excited at the same time.

"What are you doing here?" shouted Max. "What do you want with the man and the woman?"

"I'm torturing them to death."

"We can give you want you want. Name it."

"I don't need anything."

Max didn't understand. But he didn't have to. All there was to know that this man couldn't be bought. Otherwise he would have had a demand ready. Otherwise he would have acted completely differently.

"Max, is that you?" It was his brother's voice.

Max didn't respond. He didn't want to give the stranger too much information.

"You're all alike," shouted the stranger. "Your emotions get you killed. I assume you're friends, maybe relatives.

One comes looking for the other. It's the oldest story in the book. And I'm the spider, just waiting patiently. You can't fool a spider. Now come out from behind that tree with your hands up. I won't shoot you."

"What will you do?" shouted Max. He wanted to know more about this man's mind. His intentions.

"Nothing. Absolutely nothing."

"Don't believe him, Max!" shouted John.

"He's torturing us to death!" shouted Cynthia.

"Don't think I'm going to believe that. That you'll do nothing."

"Are you trying to prove you're a little smarter than the rest of them? These two fell right into my trap."

"You want to torture me?"

"That's right."

The stranger's voice sounded like it was getting closer. Was he trying to sneak up on Max?

"If you come out," shouted the man, "what I'll promise you is that it'll take me a long time to kill you. One of your other friends might come to rescue you. It'll work for both of us. I get to be the spider and catch another fly. You'll get to hold out hope as you die."

"No good," shouted Max.

"That's disappointing."

The voice was closer.

Max knew now he was dealing with someone with an altered mind. He had to approach the stranger on that same level. He had to appeal to something inside him.

"I've got a proposition," shouted Max.

Silence.

But no footsteps nearby. The stranger wasn't dangerously close. Not yet. Was he trying to sneak up on Max or wasn't he?

Max charged ahead with his plan, thinking rapidly as the words tumbled out of his mouth. "We fight. You and me. No guns. No knives."

"We're already fighting!" Laughter roared out of the man. It was chilling laughter, as cold as the air.

"You want to inflict pain, right?"

Silence.

"You don't want to shoot me. At least, not kill me. Otherwise I have a feeling I'd already be dead. You're a good shot, but you've been missing on purpose." Max didn't know if it was true, but flattering never hurt. "What I'm saying is you against me. A personal experience. Personal pain."

Max's throat was sore from shouting so much.

Still silence.

"Fine. You're not like the others. You understand me."

"Let's just get this over with. Your hostages will confirm whether you have a gun or not."

"What about you?"

"I'll toss everything into the snow."

Max knew he might have been making a huge mistake. He tossed the rifle away from him, into the snow, where it'd be visible from the stranger's point of view. Without his rifle, he'd be at a disadvantage if it came to another long-distant firefight. But he was already at a disadvantage.

Silence. Some distant footsteps.

"He's put the gun down. Twenty feet away. His handgun too. He's got a knife still. He's putting the knife down. Ten feet away. To the east." John was shouting out all the information he could.

Apparently Max had read the stranger right.

"Don't do this, Max!" shouted Cynthia. "He's some kind of monster. Don't trust him."

Max didn't answer.

"He's standing behind a tree," shouted John. "He's waiting for you. I don't know if he's armed. He might have had a hidden gun."

A flurry of noise, footsteps. Max heard a strange sound. And screaming. Horrible screaming.

Max stepped out from behind the tree, moving rapidly, running towards the stranger, his brother, and Cynthia.

The stranger was bent over one of the bodies. Probably John. Blood was on his hand. Blood was on the snow.

Max threw himself onto one knee, partially covered by a tree, his Glock in both hands held out straight in front of him.

The stranger had a handgun too.

But Max was faster.

He squeezed the trigger once. Twice. A third time.

The stranger went down.

"He's down!" It was Cynthia.

John was moaning in pain.

Max walked forward slowly, aiming the Glock at the stranger, who was on the ground. He was making small sounds. Blood poured out from his body onto the snow.

He wasn't yet dead.

Max aimed, his gun arm stretched down at an angle, and pulled the trigger.

32

JOHN

John sat there, at the edge of camp, with the remains of his ear throbbing. The pain had dulled somewhat.

Max had cut John and Cynthia loose. The three of them had taken all the gear they could carry and left the body there in the snow. When they'd gotten to Mandy on the way back, they'd had to make a stretcher to carry her back on. She was sleeping now, as were most of the rest of them. Only Georgia, Mandy, and John were still awake, keeping watch. Georgia was on the other end of camp, hidden in the woods.

"The aspirin doing anything?" said Max. He was fiddling with the radio John had brought, adjusting the knobs. So far there'd been nothing but static.

"Not much. I wish we had something stronger."

"Maybe it's good we don't."

"What's that mean?"

"Nothing," said Max. "But caffeine might help."

"It relieves pain?"

"I read something about it," said Max, in an offhand

way. John knew that meant that Max knew what he was talking about, but didn't see the need to go too much into it.

"Never would have thought of it."

"I'll get you some coffee. We need to save the caffeine pills."

"Max, wait, I need to..."

"What?"

"I just wanted to say... I don't know. I'd be dead if it wasn't you. I've got to admit, I was starting to doubt you. But you're the reason we're all alive."

Max shook his head. "I'm not the reason," he said. "The truth is, I'd be dead if I were on my own."

"But you keep risking your life trying to save everyone else."

"You don't get it," said Max. "The only way we're going to get through this thing is with each other. All of us."

"Sounds kind of cheesy," said John. "But I guess it's true."

Max nodded.

"I still don't think you'd be dead though. You're made of tougher stuff than that."

"It could happen," said Max. "I'm sure it will at some point. Haven't you read how long people lived in hunter gatherer times?"

"About forty, right?"

"The average is low," said Max. "So you've got to imagine that a lot died well before whatever the number was. And that was before guns, back when the population was minuscule compared to now. The population must be thinning out, judging from what I saw, and what you've told me about the city. But, still, it's dense compared to any other historical period."

John didn't know what to say. "Hell of a thought," was all he could muster. He was exhausted, and he felt like he'd never been rested. Sleep was only a memory.

John turned his hand over, and examined the fingers on his left hand, where the nails had been pulled off with pliers. It still hurt like hell. Cynthia, fortunately, hadn't gotten the plier treatment. Just a couple light cuts on her skin.

"That guy was really something, right?" said John. "He didn't make sense. Nothing about him made sense."

"Well," said Max. "It made sense to him. That's all that mattered."

"He was just nuts."

"Yeah. And there are more out there like him. You saw those prison tattoos just like I did. But not just people who were in prisons, but the ones who roamed free, but were hemmed in by society. Now the world is nothing but a playground. No rules. Nothing to stop them."

"You really know how to cheer someone up."

A voice suddenly cut through the radio's static. "Help... help... Is anyone out there?"

John and Max exchanged a look.

The voice had faded out. Nothing but static.

"Did you change it? The station?"

"No," said Max.

"What happened, then?"

"I don't know. But we've got to keep listening."

* * *

ABOUT RYAN WESTFIELD

Ryan Westfield is an author of post-apocalyptic survival thrillers. He's always had an interest in "being prepared," and spends time wondering what that really means. When he's not writing and reading, he enjoys being outdoors.

Contact Ryan at ryanwestfieldauthor@gmail.com

Made in the USA
Lexington, KY
31 March 2018